THE ROYAL HOUSE OF KAREDES

Large Print Collection

TWO CROWNS, TWO ISLANDS, ONE LEGACY

*The islands of Adamas
have been torn into two rival kingdoms
by the royal family's lust for power.
But can passion reunite them?*

8 addictive large print volumes

MARCH 2010

Billionaire Prince, Pregnant Mistress
by Sandra Marton

The Sheikh's Virgin Stable-Girl
by Sharon Kendrick

APRIL 2010

The Prince's Captive Wife
by Marion Lennox

The Sheikh's Forbidden Virgin
by Kate Hewitt

MAY 2010

The Greek Billionaire's Innocent Princess
by Chantelle Shaw

The Future King's Love-Child
by Melanie Milburne

JUNE 2010

Ruthless Boss, Royal Mistress
by Natalie Anderson

The Desert King's Housekeeper Bride
by Carol Marinelli

BILLIONAIRE PRINCE, PREGNANT MISTRESS

Sandra Marton

 MILLS & BOON®

First published in Great Britain 2009
Large Print Edition 2010
Harlequin Mills & Boon Limited,
Eton House, 18-24 Paradise Road, Richmond, Surrey TW9 1SR

© Harlequin Books S.A. 2009

ISBN: 978 0 263 21635 6

BILLIONAIRE PRINCE, PREGNANT MISTRESS

Special thanks and acknowledgement are given to Sandra Marton
for her contribution to *The Royal House of Karedes* series.

Harlequin Mills & Boon policy is to use papers that are natural,
renewable and recyclable products and made from wood grown in
sustainable forests. The logging and manufacturing process conform to
the legal environmental regulations of the country of origin.

Printed and bound in Great Britain
by CPI Antony Rowe, Chippenham, Wiltshire

Sandra Marton wrote her first story when she was seven years old and began to dream of becoming a writer. Today, Sandra is the author of more than thirty romance novels. Readers around the world love her strong, passionate heroes and determined, spirited heroines.

The mother of two grown sons, Sandra lives with her husband in a sun-filled house, in a quiet corner of Connecticut, where she alternates between extravagant bouts of gourmet cooking and takeaway pizza.

For MM, my very own hero, yesterday, today, forever. And for MIM, whose spirit of adventure is an inspiration. I love you both.

CHAPTER ONE

PRINCE ALEXANDROS KAREDES, second in line to the throne of the Kingdom of Aristo, did not like to be kept waiting.

Indeed, he never was.

Who would be so foolish as to let a man like him cool his heels?

His own father, Alexandros thought with a sigh of resignation as he strode past the marble fireplace outside the throne room for what had to be the tenth time in as many minutes. The hands on the French ormolu clock that graced the mantel stood upright at six. Alexandros had been told the king would see him at five-thirty but Aegeus was not known for promptness, even with his children.

"An unfortunate habit," Queen Tia called it, but Alex was not as kind. He knew his father well; he was certain Aegeus's chronic lateness was yet another subtle way of reminding everyone, family included, that, though he was getting on in years, he was still king.

It was undoubtedly the same reason he'd asked Alex to meet him here, in such formal surroundings, rather than in the privacy of the royal apartments.

That was just the way it was. There was no point in questioning it. Aegeus was a more than competent ruler. He led the people of Aristo well but he had always been distant in his dealings with his wife, sons and daughters.

Alex had no objection. At six or seven, a display of affection, a lessening of formalities might have meant something, but he was thirty-one now, he had created his own eminently successful life by bringing ever-increasing international recognition and resources to the kingdom.

He had no need for signs of affection from his father. Affection was for puppies and kittens, not grown men.

Alexandros glanced at the clock again.

Even though he understood the reason for it, being kept waiting was irritating. And inconvenient. The meeting with his father would not take long. He knew that from past experience. He'd just returned from a business trip to the Far East. Aegeus would simply want to know if things had gone well, if new banks and corporations would be joining the impressive list of those already on Aristo, but he would not wish to hear the details.

Results were all that mattered, was Aegeus's motto. How one got to those results was immaterial.

That was okay with Alex. He didn't need pats on the back any more than he needed signs of affection. It was only that if the king kept him waiting much longer, he'd be late getting into town.

Not that it mattered.

His new Ferrari would easily conquer the narrow roads that wound along the cliffs looming above the Mediterranean. And even if he arrived at The Grand Hotel in Ellos past the time he'd told his date he'd pick her up, she would not complain.

A little smile lifted the corners of his lips.

Why be unduly modest? He did well with all the things he most enjoyed. Beautiful women, fast cars, baccarat, the vast business empire he'd created here and in New York.

His smile faded.

Actually, he had not done as well with women lately.

Not that they weren't his for the taking. The

woman waiting for him tonight was what the world called a supermodel. Simone had been doing a *Vogue* cover shoot outside the casino just as Alex had arrived to discuss the casino's expansion with its manager, but that had not kept him from pausing to admire the leggy blonde posing on the wide marble steps, dressed in a silk gown that clung like a second skin.

Their eyes had met. Alex had grinned and without hesitation she'd come down the steps, hips swaying thanks to heels so high they seemed to be made for sin, oblivious to the frenzied 'Hey!' of the photographer.

"Hello," she'd cooed when she had reached him, smiling the smile that was worth ten thousand dollars an hour to an advertiser. "I'm free this evening, Your Highness, and I certainly hope that you are, too."

He'd said he was leaving for Tokyo but he'd be back in three days. "Call me," she'd purred, and he had, first thing this morning. What man wouldn't? She was stunning. Sexy as hell. He knew she'd be in his bed at the apartment he kept in town before the night ended…

So what?

A crazy thought. But there it was. A gorgeous woman, another hot liaison and all he could think was, So what? He'd have the model and, come morning, she'd be looking for a way to turn a night into an affair.

He'd be looking for a polite way to make it clear he wasn't interested.

Lately, ending an affair before it really had time to start had become a pattern. He liked sex. Liked women. Their feel, their scent, their company. It was just that he couldn't seem to concentrate on any one woman lately. For weeks now, he'd drifted from one to another.

He knew damned well there were men who'd find that exciting.

He didn't.

Not that he believed in long-term affairs. A month. Two. Three, that was about it and then he'd do the right thing, send an incredibly expensive gift and move on.

Alex frowned.

The past couple of months, the only part of that familiar plan he seemed to get right was the part about moving on.

His brothers had noticed. They'd taken to teasing him about what they called his wanderlust. *With the emphasis on 'lust,'* Sebastian said, while Andreas grinned. Even his sisters got in on the act, Lissa long-distance from Paris, Kitty sighing dramatically and saying, *Poor Alex. He just can't find a woman to love.*

Well, no. He wasn't about to explain the difference between love and lust to either of them but, of course, love had nothing to do with it. Why would it? Love was one of those things people talked about that didn't really exist.

Myths. Myths as creative as any of the tall tales his long-ago Greek and Roman ancestors had believed.

What people called 'love' was hormonal nonsense—though he couldn't call what had drawn his parents together hormonal. They had come together because it was necessary. Carrying on a name, a bloodline that had existed for centuries was in the destiny of royals.

It would surely be the same for Sebastian, heir to the throne, when the time came. Sebastian would get to choose his own wife—this was the twenty-first century, after all—but he would make that choice from a carefully vetted list of acceptable young women.

Alex, second in line, would be under somewhat less pressure but he knew the responsibility of marriage to an appropriate bride, then children to bear his name, was in his future. It was all part of his duty to the house of Karedes.

He would demand only that his future wife be attractive. Beyond that, he had no expectations. Companionship, passion—those things he would find in a mistress. He would be discreet; he would never deliberately do anything to insult the woman he married but a royal wife would understand that her role was to bear him children.

Neither of them would be foolish enough to look for love. Discretion in their extra-marital affairs would be enough.

Alex stopped pacing, jammed his hands into his trouser pockets and stared at the coat of arms on the wall over the enormous fireplace.

There had been a woman once, years ago. A girl, really. He'd thought—never mind what he'd thought. What mattered was what *she* had thought, that she could use her kisses, her touch, her soft whispers to bewitch him. He'd been a boy then, led around by a part of his anatomy that had nothing to do with his brain, but he'd learned the truth about her in time and had been wiser for it.

Since then, he had not let a woman lure him into complacency. Into forgetting that a man always had to look beyond a beautiful face to see a woman's true agenda…

Until that night two months ago.

A night when a stranger had stepped into his arms, her face radiant with seeming innocence. She'd lifted her mouth to his, parted her lips to the whisper of his breath, the thrust of his tongue and the world had blurred—until the next morning, when he'd learned it had all been a lie.

"Prince Alexandros."

Not just a lie. Alex's jaw tightened. A scam. A fraud. A swindle of the first magnitude, and he had fallen for it.

"Sir? The king and queen ask that you join them."

But she hadn't gotten away with it. Instead, he'd pretended he knew nothing of her deception. She had played a part; in the harsh light of day, it had been his turn to play one, too.

He'd taken her back to bed. Had sex with her again. And that time, when it was over and she lay sated beneath him, he'd watched her eyes fill with shock as he told her he knew who she was, what she was, and promised her that all that would come of her despicable game was defeat.

Then he'd sent her packing.

The incident had meant so little to him that he could not even remember her name. Despite her wiles, he'd been the victor. He'd had hours of sex that had seemed incredible, though he knew now it had only been, well, sex. And the moment of sweet revenge that followed had made everything right.

"Your Highness? Their majesties will see you now."

Or had it?

It wasn't just women he'd had a lot of these past weeks; it was everything. He'd put endless miles on the royal private jets with business trips from his offices in New York and Aristo to Bermuda. To the Bahamas. To the Virgin Islands, to Florida, to Mexico and, most recently, Japan. Successful trips, all of them, but he'd set one hell of a pace. Meetings by day; by night, the baccarat tables, high-stakes poker…

And sex.

Was it possible he'd spent the last weeks going from country to country, bed to bed, trying to wipe away the ugly memories of a night when he'd come as close as a man could to letting a woman use him?

"Sir. The king and queen are waiting for you."

Alex blinked. Galen, his father's major-domo, stood at stiff attention before him. From the expression on his face, he'd been there a while.

"Thank you, Galen. *Efcharisto*."

"Are you well, sir?"

"Yes, yes, I'm fine. A little distracted." Alex forced a grin. "There's a lady waiting for me in town. You know how that is."

Galen permitted himself a small smile. "I am sure the lady is happy to wait, sir," he said, and stepped aside with a deep bow as Alex walked past him into the throne room.

His parents were not alone.

A handful of aides hovered around his father, who was seated at an antique desk liberally strewn with sheets of paper. His mother stood on the throne platform, encircled by several of her ladies-in-waiting who held lengths of silk brocade against her while a seamstress sat on the floor, pinning and tucking and doing whatever in heaven's name women did with all those yards and yards of fabric.

Alex's lips twitched.

Despite its elegance, the frescoes, the ceiling painted by a sixteenth-century master and a wall hung with exquisite Byzantine icons, right now the room looked more like someone's slightly messy sitting room than a place in which the kingdom's most formal ceremonies were held.

His father looked up. "There you are," he said in a tone that suggested it was he who'd been kept waiting. "Well, what do you think?"

Alex raised his eyebrows. "About what?"

"About these plans, of course." Aegeus slapped a hand on the papers spread over his desk. "Do we want a theme, or do we not?"

No, Alex thought, this was not someone's sitting room, this was more like the Mad Hatter's tea party.

"A theme for what?" he said carefully.

Aegeus shot to his feet, scattering the aides crowded around him.

"For your mother's sixtieth birthday celebration, of course! If you hadn't spent the last month doing God knows what, you'd know what was going on here!"

"Now, Aegeus." Husband and son looked at the queen, who smiled at them both. "You know Alexandros has been busy convincing foreigners that our kingdom is the perfect place for them to invest in the future. And I'm sure we can assume he's been successful. Haven't you, Alex?"

Alex smiled and went to his mother. She bent toward him and he took her hand and brought it to his lips.

"Mother. I've missed you."

"How was your trip?"

"It was fine." Alex smiled. "We snared a lot of foreigners who look forward to a happy future."

His mother laughed. "You see, Aegeus? It's just as I said." Tia waved the women away and came gracefully down the steps. "It's good to have you home again, Alexandros."

"It's good to be here." Alex nodded at the women gathering up the fabrics. "What's all this?"

"I just told you what it is," Aegeus said with impatience. "Preparation for your mother's birthday celebration. I thought we should make the final selections of décor, color and fabric here in the throne room, where the most formal part of the ceremony will take place. Isn't that right, gentlemen?"

The aides nodded.

"We want to be certain everything comes together properly."

Aegeus looked at his aides, who nodded again. Alex thought of turkeys pecking for grain at the feet of the farmer who owned them and repressed a smile.

"So, what do you think, Alexandros? What theme shall we use? Our history as part of the ancient world? A link to the days of the Crusades? The time of the Ottoman Empire? All those things, as you well know, are in our bloodline."

Who gave a damn? What mattered was the celebration of his mother's sixtieth birthday, not his father's lineage.

"Any of those would be fine," Alex said smoothly, with a quick glance at his mother. "Something big and splashy. After all, we don't want it said that only the Calistans can do parties that are showy."

He saw his mother bite back a smile. Any mention of Calista, which had once been part of the Adamas empire along with Aristo, was enough to make his father's hackles rise.

"Showy," Aegeus said, frowning.

"Exactly." Alex shook his head. "I've never understood why there was so much coverage of the Queen of England's birthday celebration a couple of years ago when it was all so low-key. Have you, Mother?"

"No," Tia said with perfect innocence, "I've never understood it, either. All those reporters and television people, the worldwide interest in Elizabeth and the British royals…and all of it done, as you say, Alexandros, with such quiet elegance."

The king snorted. "What is there to understand? One either knows the virtue of simplicity or one doesn't." He looked down at the papers on his desk, studied them for a long moment, then swept them to the floor with his hand. "I have just chosen a theme for your birthday celebration, Tia. The coming of spring. I can envision it now. Masses of early spring flowers. The Venetian dinnerware in shades of palest green and yellow. And you, the queen, dressed in a gown the same pale pink as the diamond in the Aristan crown."

Thank you, Tia mouthed to her son. Alex flashed her a grin.

"That sounds very nice," she said demurely.

"Nice? It will be magnificent, especially with you resplendent in the new necklace I'll commission as your birthday gift. Although we could add a brooch…"

"No brooch," the queen said. "It would be inappropriate, Aegeus, to wear both a brooch and a necklace."

The king waved his hand. "Whatever. Take it up with the craftsman."

"The jewelry designer," Tia commented. "That's what she is."

She? Alex frowned and thought back to the weekend the final half-dozen jewelry designers, selected from all around the globe, had been invited to Aristo to meet with his parents. Had there been another woman in the group? He only recalled one.

But then, he thought grimly, that had been the

plan, hadn't it? That the prince who might influence the choice of designer should have been so bewitched he would notice only one?

Besides, what did his father mean by talking about the necklace he would commission? The commission had been made weeks before.

"—don't you agree, Alexandros?"

Alex looked at his father. "Sorry, Father. I missed that."

"I said, it doesn't matter what this woman is called. Designer, artisan, craftsman—crafts-*woman*," the king amended, with a nod to his wife. "She simply must understand the importance of this commission... And why are all the rest of you still hanging about?" Aegeus clapped his hands and the seamstress, aides and ladies-in-waiting scurried from the room. "She must understand that, Tia. That is a given."

The queen nodded. "I am certain that she will."

"I hope you're right. She seemed very young to me."

Things were becoming more confusing. His parents were definitely referring to a woman designer. A young designer... Alex stiffened.

No. They couldn't be talking about her. About Maria Santos and, yes, he damned well did remember her name. How could he not? A man who was marked to be the gullible victim of a scam didn't forget the person who'd been the scammer.

"She couldn't have seemed anything to you, Aegeus," Tia said, with a little smile. "Remember? We never had the pleasure of meeting her. She sent us a note and explained she'd been taken ill that morning. But, of course, we already had seen Miss Santos's sketches, and—"

A fist seemed to clench Alex's gut. He took a deep breath and forced himself to speak calmly. "Maria Santos? But you said the commission went to a French company."

"It did, but they just notified us that the owner passed away and left the firm tied up in all kinds of unpleasant litigation." Tia took Alex's arm. "I know. It's all very last minute, and Miss Santos doesn't even know that we're going to ask her to implement her design."

"That's why your trip to New York has such urgency, Alexandros."

Alex stared at his father. "What trip to New York?"

"You will see the Santos woman and inform her of our decision."

"What your father means," Queen Tia said, "is

that you'll explain what's happened and ask Miss Santos if she will be generous enough to take on the job at such short notice."

Another snort from the king. "She'll leap at the chance."

"But she might not," the queen said softly. "This is very last minute. And true artists have tender egos. Miss Santos may not like thinking of herself as second choice."

Alex wanted to laugh. A tender ego? He'd bet Maria Santos had an ego that could dent cast iron.

"You're the diplomat in the family," the king said briskly. "All that talking and contracting with the businesses you've lured to our island over the years…"

It was as close to a compliment as his father had ever offered but it wasn't enough to make Alex go to Maria Santos and present her with the chance of a lifetime.

"I would be happy to help," Alex said briskly, "but I have pressing commitments here on the island. Surely someone else can—"

"Someone else cannot," Aegeus retorted. "You have offices and an apartment in New York. You know the city. You know its tempo, its attitude. You'll be better able to work with the Santos woman and ensure the necklace is ready in time."

So much for compliments. This was a royal command. That the woman who'd wanted this job badly enough to damned near sell herself to secure it would now get it by default, that he would be the man who'd have to offer it to her, was almost too ironic to believe.

"There were other designs submitted," he said. "Surely one of them would do?"

His mother's small hand tightened on his arm. "I preferred Miss Santos's work from the beginning, Alex. I deferred to your father when he selected the French firm, of course, but now…"

Alex looked at the queen as her words trailed away. He knew it would take little for his father to tell her he had decided on a different designer. Tia was as restrained as Aegeus was quick-tempered, as gentle as the king was stern. He'd always had the feeling his mother's life was not quite the life she had hoped for.

Growing up, he'd spent little time at her side. Boarding school, tutors, the expected rigor of life as a king's son had seen to that, but he loved her deeply none the less. And if a birthday gift designed by Maria Santos was what she wanted…

"Alexandros?" Tia said softly. "Do you think I'm making a mistake?"

Alex put his arm around his mother's shoulders and hugged her.

"What I think is that you should have precisely what you want on your birthday."

His mother beamed. "Thank you."

"Thank *me*, you mean," the king said briskly, and gave his wife what passed for a loving smile. "I'm the one commissioning your gift."

The queen laughed. She rose on her toes and kissed her son's cheek, then reached for her husband's hand.

"Thank you both," she said. "How's that?"

"It's fine," Alex replied.

And that was what he kept telling himself, that it would be fine, during the seemingly endless flight all the way from Aristo to New York.

CHAPTER TWO

EVERYTHING was going to be fine.

Absolutely fine, Maria told herself wearily as the Lexington Avenue local rumbled to a stop at the Spring Street subway station.

Never mind that the man next to her smelled like a skillet of sautéing garlic. Forget that her feet were shrieking after a day strapped into gorgeous-but-impossible Manolo stilettos. Pretend the rain that had become sleet hadn't turned her sleek, three hundred dollar *Chez Panache* blow-out right back into her usual tumble of coffee-colored wild curls, or that she was obviously coming down with the flu or something suspiciously like it.

Oh, yes, everything was going to be fine.

And if it wasn't…if it wasn't…

The train gave a lurch as it left the station. Garlic Man fell into her, Maria stumbled sideways and felt one of her sky-high heels give way.

A word sprang to her lips. It was a word ladies didn't use, even if they knew how to say it in

Spanish as well as English. Not that Maria felt much like a lady right now. Still, she bit back the word, instead visualized it in big neon letters and decided that trying to figure a way to find the lost heel on the floor of the packed subway car was something only a madwoman would attempt.

Goodbye, Manolo Blahniks. Goodbye, Chez Panache. Goodbye, Jewels by Maria.

No. Absolutely, no. She was not going to think like that. What was it she'd learned in that stress reduction class? Okay, she hadn't taken the class, not exactly; there was no time for anything like taking classes in her life but she'd read the course description in The New School catalog…

Live in the now.

That was it. Reduce stress by learning to live in the now. At the moment, that meant—*damn!*— that meant the train was pulling into Canal Street.

"Excuse me. Sorry. Coming through!"

She pushed her way through the rush-hour crowd, reached the doors just as they began to shut and hurled herself onto the platform. The doors closed; the train started. People surged toward the stairs, carrying a hobbling Maria in their midst.

Climbing the steps to the street with one shoe

now four inches shorter than the other was an interesting experience. Why did they make shoes with heels like these? Better still, why had she bought them? Because men thought they looked good? Well, they did, but that wasn't the reason. There was no man in her life; she couldn't imagine there would be, not for a long time after that incident two months ago on Aristo.

The prince. The prince of darkness, was how she'd taken to thinking of him, and she felt the anger rise inside her again.

Damn it, why was she remembering him, anyway? Why waste time on him or that night? It had all been a nightmare. She hated herself for it, would probably always hate herself for it, thought not half as much as she hated him and…

And, there was no point in this.

Aristo, the commission she'd wanted so much and lost because of him, were behind her. She had to concentrate on the present. On how to convince shops like *L'Orangerie* to buy her designs.

That, she thought grimly, *that* was why she'd worn these shoes. Why she'd spent as much on a stupid blow-out as she could have spent to buy gold wire for the new earrings she'd been sketching. Why she'd all but begged for today's meeting with the buyer from *L'Orangerie*. And where had it gotten her?

Nowhere, Maria thought as she reached the sidewalk. Nowhere except out here, limping home like a derelict in sleet that was rapidly turning to snow.

The weather, coupled with the fact that it was Friday, had sent people fleeing their offices earlier than usual. Still, the street was crowded. This was Manhattan, after all. The good news was that because this *was* Manhattan, nobody so much as looked at her.

Still, she felt ridiculous, hobbling like this.

Yes, Maria, but the better news is that your heel could have come off when you were on Fifth Avenue, heading for that meeting with the man from L'Orangerie.

What an impression she'd have made then.

Not that it would have mattered.

L'Orangerie's head buyer had been polite enough to keep the lunch appointment and honest enough to begin it by telling her he wasn't going to buy her designs.

"I like them, Ms. Santos," he'd said, "I like them very much—but your name will mean nothing to our clients. Perhaps after you've had a bit more exposure…?"

More exposure? Maria gave an inelegant snort as she turned the corner. How much more exposure did she need? After winning the Caligari prize, she'd sold to Tiffany's. To Harry Winston. To Barney's.

She'd said all that to her luncheon companion. And *he* had said yes, he knew she had, but her status in those places was insignificant compared to designers like Paloma Picasso and Elsa Peretti, *n'est-ce pas*?

Not, she'd wanted to say. Not *n'est-ce pas*.

Maybe she didn't have a lot of pieces in the display cases. Maybe the stores didn't buy whole page ads for her in *The New York Times* and the high fashion magazines. Okay, maybe they didn't advertise her name at all.

But she'd sold to the big players. That mattered. And the pieces she'd designed were certainly more significant than that phony French accent laid over the unmistakable under-pinnings of his Brooklyn upbringing.

She almost told him so.

Fortunately, sanity had made her put a forkful of salad instead of her foot in her mouth.

She couldn't afford to insult a jewelry buyer of such influence. The world to which she wanted entry was small. Gossipy. Insulting one of its door-keepers came under the heading of Shooting Yourself in the Head Just to See if the Gun Would Fire.

Besides, he was right.

She'd been incredibly lucky to sell a few pieces to those stores. Who knew if she'd ever sell them others? Who knew *how* she'd sell them others? Not landing the Aristan commission had been an enormous setback.

When you could add a discreet line to your business card that said 'By commission to Their Majesties, King Aegeus and Queen Tia of Aristo,' you had the world by the tail.

She'd lost the chance to have that happen.

Correction. A man had taken that chance from her. A man who had seduced her and then tossed her out of his bed as if she'd been a twenty-dollar whore.

"Stop that," she muttered to herself. Why think of him now? Why waste time looking back? There was no point.

Maria made a left on Broome Street, hobbled to the next corner, turned down that street and, finally, there it was. Her building. Well, not hers. The building in which she lived. And worked. That was the great thing about renting a loft. There was plenty of space within its high walls, room for sleeping and eating, but mostly room for working.

If she could keep working.

The fact of the matter was, she was in debt up to her ears.

The loft cost thousands a month to rent. The gold and silver, the precious and semi-precious stones with which she worked, cost thousands, too. She had only one employee, Joaquin, but she had to meet his salary every week. And designing something that would be a fit gift for the Queen of Aristo's sixtieth birthday had taken hours and hours of time.

So she'd borrowed the small fortune she'd needed to pay her rent, her bills, to set aside other projects and devote endless hours to a design for the competition.

Useless, all of it. Useless.

She had been one of the three finalists. They'd all been invited to Aristo, where the winner would be announced at a ceremony. And she'd lost any possibility of being that winner in one night. One foolish night.

A handful of hours had ruined her hopes and dreams, had left her humiliated beyond measure and the truth was, it was her fault, all of it. Not the fault of the man who'd seduced her.

Alexandros, the Prince of Aristo, had only proved what she already knew. The hell with soft lights and sweet talk. All a man wanted from a woman was sex. That she, of all women, should have forgotten that cold truth and given in to a moment's weakness, was unforgivable.

Once you'd warmed a man's bed, he had no further use for you. If something unexpected happened, like, in this case, it turning out that he was an Aristan prince and you were a finalist in the competition to design his mother's birthday gift, he'd lay the blame for the seduction on you, even when he was the one who'd done the seducing.

Her father had put the blame on her mother.

The mighty prince had put the blame on her.

"Damn this useless shoe," Maria said furiously. To hell with the snow and the icy pavement. She bent down, ripped off both the broken shoe and its mate, and strode the last few wet yards to her front door.

It swung open just as she reached it. Joaquin stepped onto the street, smiled when he saw her but his smile changed to bewilderment as his startled gaze dropped to her nylon-clad feet.

"Maria? *¿Cuál es la materia? ¿Por qué está usted descalzo en este tiempo?*"

Maria forced a smile. "Nothing's wrong. I

broke my heel, that's all." She stepped past him into the vestibule. "I thought you'd be gone by now."

The door swung shut behind her. She started up the stairs to the loft, Joaquin at her heels. There was a freight elevator, but, as usual, it wasn't working.

"I am still here, as you can see. I waited in hopes you would return to tell me good news."

Maria nodded but said nothing. When they reached the third floor, she stabbed her key into the lock, walked briskly across the age-dulled hardwood floor, dropped her shoes and bag on a table near one of the loft's big windows and turned toward her old friend and co-worker.

"That was good of you."

Joaquin's warm brown eyes searched her face. "It did not go well?"

Maria sighed as she slipped her coat from her shoulders. She could lie or at least make the meeting with the buyer sound more hopeful, but there was no point. Joaquin knew her too well. He'd been working for her for five years. More than that, they'd grown up in neighboring apartments in a crumbling building in the Bronx, which was not a place most people thought of when they spoke of New York.

Joaquin and his family had come from Puerto

Rico to the mainland when he was five and she was six. He was the brother she'd never had.

So, no. Trying to fool him was useless.

"Maria?" he said softly, and she sighed.

"We didn't get the contract."

His expression softened. "Ah. I am so sorry. What happened? I thought this Frenchman had good taste."

"He's not even a Frenchman," Maria said with a little laugh. "As for taste, well, he says he likes my work. But—"

"But?"

"But, I should get in touch with him when Jewels by Maria is better known."

"When it is," Joaquin said stoutly, "you won't need him."

Maria grinned. "It's just a good thing you're married or I'd nab you for myself."

Joaquin grinned, too. It was an old joke and they both knew it had no meaning. So did Joaquin's wife, who was Maria's best friend.

"I'll be sure and tell Sela you said that."

"Tell her, too, that I'm looking forward to dinner on Sunday."

"I will." Joaquin tucked his hands in his overcoat pockets. "I left the new wax castings on the workbench."

"Thank you."

"FedEx delivered the opals you ordered. I put them in the safe."

"Excellent."

Joaquin hesitated. "There is also a letter—a registered letter—from the bank."

"Of course there is," Maria said sharply. She sighed and put her hand lightly on Joaquin's arm in apology. "Sorry." She smiled. "No need to kill the messenger, right?"

"You might change your mind when I tell you that your mother phoned."

Joaquin said it lightly but they both knew a call from Luz Santos was rarely pleasant. Maria's mother's life had not gone well; she held her daughter responsible. Having Maria had changed her life. It had ended her dreams. Her plans. Not that she had regrets. Oh, no. No regrets. She had sacrificed everything for Maria but that was what mothers were supposed to do.

If only Maria would make the sacrifice worthwhile. If only she would stop playing with trinkets and get a real job…

"My mother," Maria said, and sighed again. "Did she say what she wanted?"

"Her back is acting up. She has indigestion. Her doctor is of no use to her." Joaquin cleared his throat. "Mrs. Ferrara's daughter was just promoted."

Maria nodded. "Of course."

"So was your cousin Angela."

"Again," Maria said, deadpan.

"Again," Joaquin agreed.

Suddenly, it seemed too much. The day. The disappointment. The overdue bank loan. The flu symptoms she couldn't shake, and now a call from Mama... A little moan escaped her lips. Joaquin put his arms around her and she gave in and leaned her head against his shoulder.

"Maria, I have a fine idea. Come with me. You know Sela will be thrilled to see you. She is making Chile Colorado for supper. When was the last time you had something so delicious, hmm?"

She smiled, stood straight and knotted the woolen scarf at his neck.

"Joaquin," she said gently, "go home."

"If there was a way Sela and I could help you—"

"I know."

"If only you had gotten that commission. I still cannot understand the reason you didn't win."

She understood it, but she'd sooner have died than divulge it.

"You'll see, Joaquin. Everything will work out."

"De su boca al oído del Dios."

From her mouth to God's ear. It made her smile again. She clasped his face in her hands and kissed him lightly on the mouth.

"Go home, *mi amigo*."

"Sela will be angry I left you alone at a time like this."

"Tell Sela I love her but I am your boss," Maria said with mock severity, "and I sent you home."

Joaquin grinned. "Yes, boss," he said, and pressed a kiss to her forehead.

She watched as he made his way to the door. It swung shut after him and she wrapped her arms around herself and shuddered. It was very cold in the loft. The high ceiling seemed to steal the landlord's miserly allotment of heat from the radiators and the windows, though wonderfully big, were as old as the building. On a day like this, the wind was relentless and sent chilly air straight into the cavernous room.

A draft was blowing right on her. And a film of frost was just beginning to form on the glass. Maria rubbed at it with her fist…

What was that car doing here?

It was parked just across the street. A big car,

long and black and elegant. She knew little about automobiles but in this still-ungentrified stretch of Lower Manhattan a Rolls or a Mercedes or a Bentley, whatever the vehicle was, stood out like the proverbial sore thumb.

Her lips turned down.

It was probably a realtor, trying to get a feel for things. They'd been showing up as regularly as rats in the alley, a sure sign that the area was about to become too expensive for people like her. One realtor had even turned up at her door a couple of weeks ago, oozing charm. She'd only managed to get rid of him by assuring him she didn't own her loft—though she hadn't been able to keep from telling him that if she did, there wasn't a way in the world she'd sell it to him.

In a gesture of defiance and frustration, she glared at the car and stuck out her tongue. Then she drew back into the darkness, laughing nervously at herself. What a crazy thing to do but on a day that had gone as badly as this, it was better than nothing.

Alex, sitting in the back of the Bentley limo, blinked in surprise.

Had the Santos woman just stuck her tongue out at him?

No. Why would she do that? She couldn't even see him. It was dark. The windows of the car were tinted. She had no way of knowing if there was someone in the car or not.

A distortion, then, caused by the cold and the heavily falling snow.

Not that it had been falling heavily enough to have kept him from seeing that cozy lovers' greeting between her and the man who'd just left. And not that he gave a damn. Five minutes to explain why he was here, that the commission was hers, and that would be the end of it.

This was for his mother. He could ignore his anger. His disgust. He could do this.

He just wished he hadn't had to view such a charming little scene. It was enough to make his belly knot. A snowy evening. A lover, so eager for his woman that he met her downstairs. Greeted her with tenderness. Went back upstairs with her. Talked to her. Kissed her…

And walked away.

Alex frowned.

What sort of lover was this man? Why had he chosen the cold night instead of a woman's heat? As for tenderness… Did he not know that tenderness was not what Maria Santos wanted? She was hot. Wild. Eager in bed.

Even now, he could remember how she had been that night. Her scent. Lilies of the valley, he had thought, as delicate and fragrant as those that grew wild in the hills near his home on the cliffs. Her skin, warm and soft under his questing hands. Her hair, brushing like silk against his throat.

Her nipples, sweet on his tongue.

Her mouth hot, so hot against his.

Her little cries. Her moans. That one incredible moment as he'd entered her when he'd thought—when he'd imagined—that she had never before known a man's possession.

And, damn it, what in hell was he doing? His body had grown hard, just remembering. Alex let down the window and drew a long breath of cold, snow-laden air into his lungs.

The thing to remember was not how she had been in his bed but the reason she had been there. It had not been an accident; that she'd stood in seeming uncertainty just in front of the building in which he had his offices in Ellos, guidebook in hand, had been, he knew, deliberate.

He had not suspected it then.

But he'd noticed her right away. What man wouldn't?

Slender, very pretty, her dark mane of hair pulled away from her face by a simple gold clasp and left to tumble down her back, her figure limned by the fading light of the day, she'd been a delightful sight.

He'd paused as he came out the door. She had a pair of small reading glasses perched on the end of her nose; somehow, that had added to her charm.

American, he'd thought, *a tourist. And, without question, lost.*

He'd been in no particular hurry to go anywhere. *Okay, why not?* he'd said to himself, and smiled as he'd approached her. "Excuse me," he'd said pleasantly, "but do you need some help?"

She'd looked up from the slim guidebook, her eyes a little blurry because of the glasses. Her hesitation had been artful, just enough to make her seem not just cautious but almost old-fashioned.

"Well—well—thank you. Yes, actually, I do. If you could tell me… I'm looking for the *Argus*. It's a restaurant. Well, a café. The guidebook says it's supposed to be right here. The hotel desk clerk said so, too. But—"

"But it isn't," Alex had said, smiling again. "And, I'm afraid, it hasn't been, not for at least a year."

Her face had fallen. Disappointment had only made her lovelier.

"Oh. Oh, I see. Well—thank you again."

"You're most welcome."

She'd taken off her glasses and gone on looking up at him, her eyes—hazcl, he'd noted, neither brown nor green nor gold but a veritable swirl of colors—as wide and innocent as a fawn's.

Innocent as a fox approaching a hen house, he thought now, his mouth thinning to a tight line.

Maria Santos had known exactly what she was doing, right up to how she'd reacted when he'd suggested another restaurant nearby.

"Is it…?" She'd hesitated. "I mean, is this other restaurant ?"

"As good as the *Argus*?" Truth was, he had no idea. He'd never been to the *Argus*. From what little he recalled, it had been a tiny café, just a place to get a quick bite.

"As inexpensive." Color had swept into her cheeks. "The guidebook says—"

"You don't have to worry about that," he'd said, because she wouldn't.

The restaurant he'd recommended was incredibly expensive—but he would take her to it. He would dine with her and pay the bill. Just to talk, he'd told himself. Just to be a good ambassador for his country, even though—to his surprise—this beautiful stranger did not seem to recognize his face when the simple truth, much to his chagrin, was that spotting him was as much a tourist attraction as the beaches, the yachts and the casino.

The hell she hadn't recognized him.

She'd known who he was. She'd set the entire thing up.

But he had not known it, then.

She'd protested prettily that she couldn't possibly let him pay for her meal but she'd let him think he'd overcome her protests. And, after dinner, when they'd walked along the sea wall, when he'd kissed her while they stood surrounded by the tall pines that grew on a little promontory and their kisses had gone from soft and exploratory to hot and deep, when his hands had gone under her silk skirt and she'd moaned into his mouth, when he'd put his arm tightly around her waist, still kissing her, and led her through the now-quiet streets to his flat, to his bed, when she'd clung to him and whispered she'd never done anything like this before…

When she'd come apart in his arms, her cries so sweet, so wild, so real…

Alex cursed.

"Sir?" his driver said, but Alex ignored him,

swung open the door of the Bentley himself and stepped into the night.

Lies, all of it, lies that had come undone in the early morning when he'd reached for her again and found her side of the bed empty. He'd assumed she was in the bathroom.

She wasn't.

He'd heard her voice, soft as the breeze from the sea. Was she on the phone? Without knowing why he did it, he'd carefully lifted the one on his night table and brought it to his ear.

Yes, he'd heard her say with a breathy little laugh, *yes, Joaquin, I think I really do have a good chance of being named the winner. I know the competition is tough but I have every reason to believe my chances are really excellent.*

She'd looked up from the telephone when he walked into the kitchen. Her face had gone crimson.

"You're awake," she'd begun to say, with an awkward smile.

He'd taken the phone from her hand. Pressed the 'end' button. Carried her back to bed without saying a word, taken her in passion born of anger.

Then he'd told her to get her clothes on. To get the hell out. And not to bother showing up at the palace, later.

"Your chances of being named to design my mother's birthday gift," he'd said in clipped tones, "are less than those of a snowball in hell."

Alex strode across the street.

It had taken two months but that prediction was no longer just a metaphor. Here was the snow. And, in just a couple of minutes, Maria Santos would get a first-hand introduction to hell.

And he would get the satisfaction of putting her, and that night, out of his head.

Forever.

CHAPTER THREE

MARIA sighed, peeled off her dressed-for-success suit jacket, tossed it over the back of a chair and automatically reached for the phone to return her mother's call.

Her hand stilled.

What was she doing? A ten-minute litany of aches and pains, followed by a lecture about how she needed to get a real job, were the last things she wanted right now.

Get out of her clothes. Run a hot bath. Eat something. Then she'd make the call.

Maria looked at her shoes, made a face and heaved them into the big trash can beside her work table. Gorgeous but impractical. She should have known better than to have bought them. Gorgeous but impractical was not for her. It never had been.

And she hadn't bought the shoes for today, she'd bought them for the weekend she'd gone to Aristo. She'd wanted to look sophisticated, but the shoes hadn't done her much good then, either. Even if she'd looked sophisticated, she'd behaved like a—like a—

No. She wasn't going there. Not tonight. Rejected by a phony Frenchman today, rejected by an arrogant Aristan two months ago.

That was more than enough.

She stepped out of her skirt and padded, barefoot, to the end of the loft that served as a sleeping area. She tossed the skirt on the futon, peeled off her bra and pantyhose, yanked the clasp from her hair, bent forward and ran her hands briskly through the now-wildly curling strands. Then she tossed her head back, grabbed a pair of old, scruffy sweats, and put them on.

Time for supper, though the thought of eating made her feel vaguely queasy.

Nothing new in that. On top of everything else, she'd felt vaguely ill for the past week or so. No big surprise, considering that half the city was down with the flu. She probably had it, too, but she couldn't afford to give in to it right now, not with half a dozen pieces to complete by the end of the month.

Her buyers expected her to be prompt. And she needed the money they'd owe her on delivery.

So, no, she wouldn't even admit to the possibility that she might be sick. Absolutely not.

She was under stress, she was working hard. The fatigue, the heaviness in her limbs, the faint sense of nausea that came and went…

Stress, was what it was.

Something to eat, something bland, would make her feel better. Nerves had made her bypass breakfast; lunch had been a joke. Definitely, she had to put something in her stomach.

Soup? Scrambled eggs? Grilled cheese? Better still, she could order in from Lo Ming's, down on the corner. Egg drop soup. Steamed dumplings. Forget the calories. Forget the cost. An order of Chinese comfort food, then she'd turn on the TV, curl up on the sofa, get lost in something mindless while—

The doorbell rang.

Now what? It was late. Who would come here at this hour?

Of course. Joaquin. He knew what a setback today had been. He'd probably gone half a block, phoned Sela on his cell phone and she'd ordered him to go back and insist Maria come for supper.

The bell rang again. Maria pinned a smile to her lips, went to the heavy door, undid the lock and pulled it open.

"Joaquin," she said, "honestly, you have to learn to take 'no' for an ans…"

Alexandros Karedes, snow dusting the shoulders of his leather jacket and glittering like jewels in his dark hair, stood at the door. Maria felt the blood drain from her head.

"Good evening, Ms. Santos."

His voice was as she remembered it. Deep. Husky. Perfect English, but with the faintest hint of a Greek accent. And cold, as cold as it had been that awful morning she would never forget, when he'd accused her of horrible things, called her terrible names...

"Aren't you going to ask me in?"

She fought for composure. Last time they'd faced each other, they'd been on his turf. Now they were on hers. She was in command here, and that meant everything.

"There's a sign on the door downstairs," she said, her tone every bit as frigid as his. "It says, 'No soliciting or vagrants.'"

His lips drew back in a wolfish grin. "Very amusing."

"What do you want, Prince Alexandros?"

A tight smile eased across his mouth and it killed her that even now, knowing he was a vicious, arrogant man, she couldn't help but notice what a handsome mouth it was. Chiseled. Generous. Beautiful, like the rest of him, which made him living proof that beauty could, indeed, be only skin deep.

"Such formality, Maria. You were hardly so proper the last time we were together."

She knew his choice of words was deliberate. She felt her face heat; she couldn't help that but she damned well didn't have to let him lure her into a verbal sparring match.

"I'll ask you once more, Your Highness. What do you want?"

"Ask me in and I'll tell you."

"I have no intention of asking you in. Tell me why you're here or don't. It's your choice, just as it will be my choice to shut the door in your face."

He laughed. It infuriated her but she could hardly blame him. He was tall—six two, six three—and though he stood with one shoulder leaning against the door frame, hands tucked casually into the pockets of the jacket, his pose was deceptive. He was strong, with the leanly muscled body of a well-trained athlete.

She remembered his body with painful clarity. The feel of him under her hands. The power of him moving over her. The taste of him on her tongue.

Suddenly, he straightened, his laughter gone. "I have not come this distance to stand in your doorway," he said coldly, "and I am not going to leave until I am ready to do so. I suggest you stand aside and stop behaving like a petulant child."

A petulant child? Was that what he thought? This man who had spent hours making love to her and had then accused her of—of trading her body for profit?

Except, it had not been love, it had been sex. And the sooner she got rid of him, the better.

She let go of the door knob and stepped aside. "You have five minutes."

He strolled past her, bringing cold air and the scent of the night with him. She swung toward him, arms folded. He reached past her, pushed the door closed, then folded his arms, too. She wanted to open the door again but she'd be damned if she was going to get into a who's-in-charge-here argument with him. *She* was in charge, and he would surely see a tussle over the ground rules as a sign of weakness.

Instead, she looked past him at the big clock above her work table.

"Ten seconds gone," she said briskly. "You're wasting time, Your Highness."

"What I have to say will take longer than five minutes."

"Then you'll just have to learn to economize. More than five minutes, I'll call the police."

Instantly, his hand was wrapped around her wrist. He tugged her toward him, his dark chocolate eyes almost black with anger.

"You do that. And I'll tell every tabloid shark I can contact about how Maria Santos tried to buy a five-hundred-thousand-dollar commission by seducing a prince." He smiled thinly. "They'll lap it up."

She blanched, but she kept her chin up and her eyes on his.

"Don't try to scare me with lies! You can't afford that kind of gossip."

"I've learned to endure that kind of gossip, Ms. Santos. It's part of my life. Besides, I'm the righteous prince who discovered what you wanted and tossed you out on your backside." Another of those cold smiles twisted his lips. "They'll eat you alive. How do you think that will go over with the handful of reputable clients you've somehow managed to snare?"

Maria yanked her hand free. *"!Usted es un cochon!"* she hissed. *"!Un cochon malnacido!"*

"I think not. If I truly were an ill-bred pig, I would have told you exactly what I thought of you eight weeks ago instead of just throwing you out of my apartment."

Color rushed to her cheeks. She hadn't figured he understood Spanish but, then, she'd been wrong in every judgment she'd made about this man from the start.

"You did tell me," she snapped, "and now it's my pleasure to return the favor. You're down to four minutes before I call the cops. Dealing with the media will be worth it, if I can just get rid of you."

"What's the problem, Maria? Expecting your lover to return?"

"What?"

"Your lover. What did you call him that morning? Joaquin?"

Joaquin. The idea was so ludicrous she almost laughed, but laughter would take more energy than she could spare. Besides, she didn't have to explain anything.

"Joaquin is none of your business."

"You're right, of course." Alex strolled across the room to the front window and peered out at his limo, waiting at the curb across the street. "But I had a front-row seat for your little welcome home this evening. You can't blame me for being curious."

Maria rushed to the window. A front-row seat? Impossible. The Prince of Arrogance would surely not have stood in the cold and the snow, watching her window…

The big car. It was his. Furious, she swung toward her unwelcome guest.

"You were sitting out there, spying on me?"

"You might want to consider curtains," he said with lazy self-assurance.

"You—you…" She pointed a finger at the door. "Get out of my home!"

Alex didn't move. Instead, he tucked his hands in the slash pockets of his jacket and gave her a long look, starting at her feet and working slowly up to her face. She certainly wasn't dressed like a woman waiting for her lover to come back. Not in a pair of baggy sweats that had seen better days. There was a hole in one knee, what looked like a burn in the shirt just below her collarbone. Her feet were bare, her hair a wild mass of curls.

His belly knotted.

Her hair had been like that the last time he'd seen her, a tumble of long, glorious curls falling around her heart-shaped face. She'd been wearing his robe; she'd been lost in it and somehow that had made her look even sexier, maybe because he'd known, intimately, what was beneath that robe. The delicate, golden-hued skin. The small, uptilted breasts. The slim curve of her waist, the surprisingly feminine richness of her hips.

Her face had been sexy, too. Glowing eyes. Dewy skin. No make-up, not even lipstick, though her mouth had been rosy and softly swollen from his kisses.

She had looked—what did the French call it? *Déshabillé.* As if she had just come from bed.

Which she had. His bed. His bed and his possession, and that memory was enough to do more than make his belly knot. It sent a bolt of pure lust straight to his loins.

He still wanted her.

It had taken the sight of her in a scruffy sweatshirt and baggy sweatpants before he'd permitted himself to admit it. What man wanted to acknowledge he still desired a woman who'd tried to use him?

One who was a fool, he told himself. And then he thought, no. Hell, no. That wasn't it at all. Maria Santos owed him and that was her fault, not his. She had lured him into bed. Seduced him, though he'd thought he was the one doing the seducing.

She'd plotted everything, from that supposedly accidental meeting on the street to the moment he'd first kissed her. The only thing surprising about that night was that shc'd been able to keep from smirking triumphantly when he'd asked her to come home with him.

She'd made a fool of him, and she still owed him for that. Owed him big time, as the Americans said. And until that debt was paid, the memory of his humiliation would continue to haunt him.

He had no doubt what it would take to expunge that memory.

Her, in his bed again. Moving bcneath him. Coming on a long, explosive cry as he watched her with clinical detachment. There'd be no phony little cries. No subterfuge. He would make her want him, make her react to him.

And then he'd send her packing for the second, and last, time.

"Your five minutes are up, Prince Alexandros."

Alex looked at her. Her expression, her body language, were defiant. She thought she was in charge.

That made him smile.

"You find this amusing?"

"Indeed."

Her eyes narrowed. "I'm going to count to

ten. It's your last chance. If you're not out the door by then—"

"*Safir et Fils* is on the verge of collapse."

She blinked. "Who?"

"*Safir et Fils,*" he repeated impatiently. "The French firm that was awarded the commission." She was staring at him blankly. "Come on, Ms. Santos," he said silkily. "Don't try and tell me the name of the company that won a commission you were willing to prostitute yourself to get has slipped your—"

Her hand flew through the air but he was quicker than she was. He caught her wrist, dragged her forward and hauled her to her toes.

"Do not," he said with quiet menace, "*ever* raise your hand to me again!"

"Let go of me!"

"Did you hear what I said?—"

"What a bastard you are!"

Her voice shook; tears glittered in her eyes and she was breathing hard. So what? He was unimpressed.

"Playing the righteous innocent will get you nowhere, *agapi mou.* You made a fool of me once but I promise you, it will never happen again. And do not call me names. I am a prince. I urge you to remember that."

He almost winced. He sounded like an ass but how could he think while hot rage pumped through his blood? She was an excellent actress; he knew that. And this was another stellar performance. The damp eyes. The trembling voice. The patches of crimson on her face.

Her face. Beautiful, even now.

"Did you think you could get away with what you did, Maria? Letting me think you'd been carried away by passion when what carried you away was the greedy hope that sleeping with me would give you an advantage in the design competition?"

He paused. Maria stared at him.

Was he waiting for her to answer? What was the point? If she said he was wrong, he wouldn't believe her. He hadn't, that awful morning.

"Liar," he'd said, in a voice cold as death, and then he'd hurled words at her in Greek that she hadn't understood, though their meaning had been painfully clear.

Trying to make him listen now would not only be pointless, it would be demeaning.

The truth was, she hadn't even known who he was that night. A prince? The son of Queen Tia and King Aegeus? As far as she'd known, he was just a man. A gorgeous, incredibly sexy, fascinating stranger whose smile, whose touch had made her breathless.

When he'd kissed her and the kisses hadn't been enough, when he'd touched her and those touches weren't enough, she'd forgotten everything—that they were in a public place, that she was a moral woman, that she had never been with a man before.

And when he'd whispered, *Come with me,* she had gone with him. How could she have done anything else?

Her world had been reduced to him. To his mouth. His hands. His hard, flagrantly aroused masculinity. She still couldn't believe she'd let such a thing happen. You didn't sleep with a stranger. *She* didn't, anyway.

"What's the matter, sweetheart? Is that busy little brain of yours trying to come up with an answer that will satisfy me?" His voice roughened. "Don't waste your time. There's only one thing that will satisfy me, and you know what that is."

What he meant was in his eyes.

She saw it and stumbled back. He could see the beat of her pulse in the hollow of her throat. Good, he thought coldly. This time, at least, he had the advantage. Command had slipped from her hands to his and she hadn't even heard the worst of what he'd come to tell her.

"Get out."

She spoke in a papery whisper that he ignored. Instead, he turned his back and walked to her work table. Sketches were tacked to an enormous corkboard on the wall above it. Something that looked as if it had been molded from wax stood on a shelf.

"Didn't you hear me? I said—"

"Didn't *you* hear *me*?" He swung toward her, arms folded, feet crossed at the ankles. "*Safir et Fils* are going under."

"Do you expect me to weep for them?"

"They will not be able to make the gift for my mother's birthday."

Her smile was pure saccharine. "Stop at Wal-Mart before you fly home."

"I know you find this amusing, Maria, but it's deadly serious. March the seventh will be an important day. My father has declared it a national holiday."

Again, that glittery smile. She had her composure back—but not for long.

"There will be a ball attended by dignitaries from around the world."

"Yes, well if you can't find anything you like at Wal-Mart—"

"My parents have chosen you to execute the commission."

Her jaw dropped. She was speechless. Twice in one evening. He had the feeling it was some kind of record.

"Me?"

"You." His mouth twisted. "You see, despite what I told you that night, I never mentioned your little game to either the king or the queen. I didn't have to. My father had chosen the French jewelers. He preferred their submission."

Maria swallowed hard. She wanted to shriek with delight but she'd be damned if she gave him that.

"How—how nice. To be second-best."

"Please. Sarcasm doesn't become you." Why mention that the queen had preferred her design all along? "We both know that this is the chance of a lifetime for a woman like you."

Her cheeks flushed again. "What, exactly, is that supposed to mean?"

"Why, only that your name, your career will be made when word gets out, Maria. What else could it possibly mean?"

She was sure that hadn't been his meaning but why argue about it? The fact was, he had it right. Orders would double. They'd triple! Tiffany would give her a window display; so would Barney's. *Vogue, Vanity Fair, Allure, Elle, Marie*

Claire…every fashion magazine in the world would camp on her doorstep and the noxious pseudo-Frenchman would be on his knees, begging her to design for *L'Orangerie.*

If only the court hadn't sent the prince to give her the news.

"They sent me," Alex said, as if he'd read her mind, "because they wanted to be sure you understood the full importance of this commission."

"You mean," Maria countered sweetly, "because the king thought your illustrious royal presence would impress me." He grinned. Her gaze on him narrowed. "Too bad your father doesn't know you as well as I do."

All at once, Alex was weary of the game. Why in hell had he ever thought he needed to settle scores? He was not a man who enjoyed revenge; God knew there was plenty of opportunity for it in business but he had always seen vengeance-seeking as a low sport. And payback against a woman, even one who really needed to be taught a lesson, suddenly held no appeal.

"What's your answer?" he said brusquely. He pushed back his sleeve, shot an impatient glance at his watch. "My pilot is standing by. Weather permitting, I want to fly home tonight."

Maria chewed on her lip. God, the man was

arrogant. If only she could tell him what he could do with his offer, but he was right. This would jump-start her career. Nothing she could ever do would match its importance. She had to say 'yes', but surely there was a way to do it so she could regain her authority.

"Very well," she said. "I'll accept the commission."

He nodded and reached into the inside breast pocket of his leather jacket.

"Good. I have some papers here…"

"There are certain conditions to be met," she said as she took the documents from him.

His dark eyebrows rose. "There are, indeed. Dates of approval. A date of completion. An agreement as to what you may and may not discuss with the media—"

"One," Maria said, "I work alone. If I need an assistant, that person will be of my choosing."

"I don't think you understand. This agreement concerns the demands of the—"

"Two, I'll need some new equipment." She smiled thinly. "Aristo's cost. Not mine."

Alex's mouth flattened. "You're fortunate to be getting this commission, Ms. Santos. Perhaps you've forgotten that."

"Three. I do not work well with anyone

watching over my shoulder. In other words, I'll be happy to show my work, as it progresses, to the king and queen at their request—but no one else."

The muscle in Alex's jaw jumped to attention. "Is that last directed at me?"

"Four," Maria said, raising her hand and ticking the point off on her finger, but he had stopped listening.

Who did she think she was, this snippet of a female? He was not of the old school; nobody had to bow to him or bend a knee in a deep curtsy, well, except, of course, on formal occasions of the court, but he *was* entitled to the respect he had been born to as a prince, the respect he had won as a man—

"If all those conditions are agreeable, I'll sign your document."

Alex didn't answer. He stood watching her from dark, unreadable eyes and felt the tension inside him growing.

He had left Aristo knowing he had to deal with Maria Santos and keep his composure. Nothing more.

Then another thought had come to him. He would bed her again. Right here. Tonight. It was he who would do the seducing this time, if not with his body then with the commission she'd so willingly sold her soul to get. He'd strip her naked, touch her everywhere, kneel between her thighs and take her again and again and again, until she was out of his system.

A moment ago, he'd come full circle. Told himself that plan was crazy. It was not him. Taking a woman out of revenge was beneath him. It was, he'd told himself, enough that she'd know she was getting the commission only because the true winner of the competition was out of the picture.

There'd been that instant of pleasure.

Then she'd taken that instant and crushed it.

Who did she think she was, to make demands of him? Of the royal court? Did she think she had the right to treat him as if he were an errand boy?

"Are you listening to me, Your Highness?"

Alex looked at her. Her eyes glittered with contempt; her very posture confirmed it. Oh yes. She saw him as an errand boy. Not her mark this time. The court's errand boy.

"I take it you heard my last stipulation," she said. "I will not deal with you after tonight. Is that clear?"

He could feel his body humming with anger.

He wanted to haul her into his arms and shake her. Humiliate her. Conquer her. Strip her of that ridiculous pair of sweats, bare her to his eyes, his hands, his mouth...

He took a step forward. Something of what he felt must have shown in his face because she paled and took a step back. *That's right,* he thought coldly. *Be afraid of me, Maria. Be afraid of what I'm going to do...*

The phone rang. She grabbed it as if it were a lifeline.

"Hello?" She listened, then cleared her throat. "Yes, *sí,* I know. Yes, I know that, too. I'm sorry you had to wait for my call." Her eyes swept to Alex; she turned her back as if that would give her the privacy she needed. "Could we discuss this another time?" she said in a low voice.

Alex had moved with her; his eyes, fixed on her, still held that dangerous glitter. Didn't he understand she needed privacy? Who did he think she was talking to? Joaquin, probably. That almost made her laugh. The voice whining in her ear was her mother's.

And hearing from Luz was the last thing she needed right now.

She turned again, desperately wishing this were a cordless phone so she could walk further away. Her mother was telling her about her cousin Angela—snide, holier-than-thou Angela—and her latest promotion at the insurance company. Maria had only to ask, Luz was saying, as she did every few weeks, and Angela would get her a job interview.

"Let me tell you my wonderful news," she said quickly, breaking into her mother's endless praise for Angela. "That commission? The one to design the birthday jewels for Queen Tia of Aristo? Well, I've landed it."

She waited, although she really didn't know what she was waiting for. She knew better than to think her mother would shriek with joy and say, *I'm so proud of you, mia bella,* or even, *That's wonderful news.* But she didn't really expect Luz to say, "You?" as if such a thing were impossible.

"You lost the competition. You were not good enough to win it."

Maria winced. "Yes. Well—well, things changed. There was a problem with the winner and so—"

"Ah." Her mother's sigh spoke volumes. "Well, no matter how you came by it, it is an opportunity. Be sure you do nothing to ruin it."

Maria felt like weeping, which was ridiculous.

Why should tonight be different than the past twenty-eight years?

What made it even worse was that Alex had not taken his eyes from her. It was infuriating. His Royal Highness was a Royal Boor when it came to manners. Didn't he know enough to walk away when someone was having a private conversation?

"One of the things your cousin Angela has always done is to make the most of her chances."

"Yes. I know." Maria cleared her throat. "It's late. I'll talk to you tomorrow."

Another deep sigh came over the phone. "God willing I will be here tomorrow. And please, Maria, do not waste time telling me the doctors say my health is excellent. What do doctors know?"

There was no point in answering. That road, well-traveled over the decades, led nowhere.

"Good night," Maria said, "I love—"

Too late. Luz had already disconnected. Maria put down the phone and swallowed hard. The Prince of Arrogance hadn't moved; he was still standing right next to her. She drew a long breath, let it out as slowly as she could, then turned to face him.

"Wasn't he interested in your charming declaration of affection?"

"Excuse me?"

"Your lover. Joaquin. I had the impression he ended the call rather abruptly. Didn't your news please him?"

"That wasn't—" She bit her lip. Would having a lover, however imaginary, offer her some protection? She needed protection; every instinct told her that. "That wasn't polite," she said. "Listening to my conversation."

He smiled thinly. "And you, Ms. Santos, are the expert on etiquette, are you not?" The smile vanished; he shoved a gold pen at her. "Sign the contract."

Why did that sound so ominous? "I insist you meet my conditions before I—"

Suddenly, his hands were on her, cupping her shoulders, lifting her to her toes.

"You're lucky to be getting this commission," he said coldly. "We both know that. You're desperate for money—please, don't waste my time denying it. And you need the prestige that comes with creating a necklace for a queen." His tone hardened. "Sign the contract, Maria."

Her lip trembled. She looked away from him and, for a heartbeat, he hated himself.

Was he really reduced to this? Bullying a woman on the skids? A woman whose lover had obviously not said a word to congratulate her on winning this commission?

And why should he give a damn? Maria Santos was nothing to him.

"Sign the papers," he growled.

She picked up the pen, smoothed out the documents, laid them on the table and scribbled her name where he indicated. He felt a surge of heat sweep through him. But he said nothing, simply took the papers, folded them and tucked them back in his pocket.

"As for conditions…there are others besides the ones I mentioned. There are *my* conditions," he said in a softly ominous tone. "And you will meet them."

His gaze dropped to her lips. She felt her pulse begin to race. Whatever he was about to say was going to turn her world upside down; she could sense it.

"One," he said, still in that soft voice, "you shall have the studio of your dreams—but on Aristo, not here."

"Are you insane? I have no intention of—"

"I assume your passport is in order."

"Of course, but—"

"You will leave with me, tonight."

"You cannot do this to—"

He bent to her and kissed her. Kissed her as if she belonged to him, his tongue in her mouth, his hands cupping her bottom, lifting her to him, into him, into the heavy thrust of his erection.

"And," he said thickly, when he finally raised his head, "you will warm my bed until you finish the job."

"No!" She shook her head as if to emphasize her refusal. "No," she said again, her voice high and wild, "I'll never—"

"You will, or I'll do what I should have done when you left my bed the first time. I'll tell the queen about our little adventure. I'll tell her you're not worthy of designing her gift or of working in proximity to her. And then you can stay in this loft and forever live with the knowledge that you failed at the one thing that could have changed your life."

Maria wanted to weep but she knew damned well her tears would have made him not just the victor but the conqueror. Instead, she forced herself to meet his gaze without flinching.

"Is this how you get your women, Your Highness? Through blackmail?"

His eyes flashed a warning. She tried to pull away but his mouth swooped down to hers; his hands swept into her hair, holding her captive to his merciless kiss until, at last, a sweet moan whispered from her throat.

Despite her fury and her hatred, it was happening again.

The hot spiral of desire she'd felt that night all those weeks ago. The sudden swift race of her heart. All those amazing, incredible feelings she'd never known before were sweeping her away.

She was dizzy in his arms, dizzy from the taste of him, the scent, the feel of his hand, now in her hair, his fingers cupping her scalp. He gathered her even closer. The hard press of his arousal dug into her belly.

Oh God. She wanted him, wanted him, wanted him…

Maria wound her arms around Alex's neck and kissed him back.

CHAPTER FOUR

SHE was on fire.

It had been like this that night on Aristo.

Alex had kissed her, and it had been like touching a match to tinder.

Until then, she'd always thought descriptions like that were clichés, the stuff of novels and movies, but Alex had taken her in his arms and taught her that a man's touch could change everything you knew, everything you believed, forever.

One kiss. One warm mingling of breath. One caress of lips and tongues and you were transformed, became someone else.

Someone you didn't know, didn't understand. Didn't respect.

Her eyes flew open. She slammed her hands against Alex's broad chest. He made a sound that was almost a growl and gathered her closer. Her struggles increased.

"Alex! Damn you, let me go."

For a moment, her words didn't penetrate. He

was lost in the taste of Maria, the feel of her soft body against his. But her hands became small fists, hammering at his shoulders. The message was clear. A moment's tease, just enough to drive him half out of his mind...

It wasn't going to work.

He opened his eyes and let go of her.

"Pack your things."

His voice was low and rough, his muscles taut with anger and frustration. She had a way of getting to him and he didn't like it. It was not something he was accustomed to.

"That's it?" Her voice shook with indignation. "You walk in here, announce that I'm going to— to be your sex slave—"

"My mistress," he said, mentally cursing himself. How had she reduced him to this?

"You think that makes it better? You cannot walk in here, manhandle me and expect— expect—"

"Is that what you call it when you turn soft and hot in a man's arms and all but beg him to take you?"

Her face colored. "Get out!"

"Try singing a different tune, *agapimeni*. The one about being a shocked virgin is getting tiresome."

"Is there something about 'get out' you don't understand?"

"And what of the contract you just signed, Maria? Shall I take that to court and have a judge deal with it?"

"Don't threaten me!"

"It's not a threat, it's a warning. You've committed to creating the queen's birthday gift, to be completed by twenty-eight February and subject to my approval."

"*Your* approval?"

"Indeed," he said coldly. "Perhaps you should have read the contract more thoroughly."

Maria wanted to laugh. Or cry. Either seemed appropriate. A minute ago, Alex had been kissing her passionately. Now, he was talking to her as if he were a prosecutor and she a balky witness.

Did he think he could use sex to control her? Or maybe he thought he could bully her. Big mistake! She'd grown up on the streets of the Bronx. What was royal arrogance compared to Bronx attitude?

"Contracts," she said, just as coldly, "are made to be broken."

Alex raised an eyebrow. "Did you lift that line from some trendy legal show?"

She flushed. Close enough. She'd taken it from an article about how a hotshot movie star had gotten away with walking out on a film.

"And you're right," he said, taking the contract from his pocket, flipping to a page and holding it out. "Some are. This one is not. Take a look at paragraph three."

Why did doing as he'd suggested smack of defeat? Was it his smug tone, or was it the instinctive knowledge that what she'd find in that paragraph would not be good? She snatched the contract from his hand, read the pertinent sentences...and felt a shock of disbelief flash through every nerve in her body.

Failure of the party of the first part to complete the agreed-upon commission and/or to fulfill the additional duties required of her in their entirety...

Her head snapped up. "What?"

"Ah," he said, his voice a low purr, "I can see that you really didn't read this before you signed it. A bad decision, I'm afraid."

"That's insane! You cannot contract for—for a mistress..."

"Keep reading," he said softly.

Did she have a choice? Her gaze dropped to the contract.

Such failure shall result in forfeiture of all

goods and services already provided and repayment for same.

"What goods and services?" She looked up and flashed a triumphant smile. "You haven't provided any."

"Have you forgotten you're flying to Aristo with me? Did you think I wouldn't provide you with a workshop and tools?" He jerked his chin toward the contract. "There's more."

Finally, in the event of forfeiture, an additional penalty to be paid by Maria Santos in the amount of...

The typed-in number had so many zeroes it made her laugh. Alex's eyes narrowed.

"I assure you, this is not meant for your amusement."

No. Of course not, but what else could she do when the penalty for walking away was easily ten times the value of everything she owned?

"You must know I can't afford anything even close to that!"

He shrugged. "I know only what is in the agreement you just signed."

He sounded as removed as if they were discussing when the snow might stop. It not only killed her hysterical laughter, it killed any hope she'd had that this was a joke.

"But—but I'd lose everything. This loft. My clients. The people I deal with would suffer, the ones who subcontract to me. And Joaquin, who's been with me from the start—"

"Your lover's welfare is not my concern."

"Joaquin is not my lover." Maria flung the contract at his feet. "He works for me."

He bent and picked it up, smoothing the pages, his expression blank.

"It doesn't matter one way or the other. My only concern is this contract. Are you going to abide by it or not?

She stared at him, hating him, hating herself even more. How could she have slept with him that night? Better still, how could she have returned his kisses just now? Was she truly, pathetically her mother's daughter?

She wanted to curse him. To pummel those broad shoulders with her fists, but what would that change? Nothing, she thought bitterly, nothing at all.

"This is usury!"

He grinned. Such a ruggedly beautiful face, she thought wildly, made even sexier by that quick devil's smile.

"An impressive legal term," he said. "But incorrect. The penalty to which you've agreed has nothing to do with a loan."

"Damn it," she exploded, "do not play word games with me! I know what usury means. And I know what this contract is. Unconscionable. Immoral. Cruel and mean-spirited and—"

"And enforceable."

"You cannot coerce a woman into—what was your phrase? Into warming your bed!"

Suddenly, he was standing much too close. She stumbled back but his big hands were already framing her face and lifting it to him.

"There's not a word that even hints of coercion in that contract," he said softly. "You signed it of your own free will."

"How can you do this?" she said shakily. "Don't you have any scruples?"

He laughed softly. "An interesting question, coming from you." His smile faded; his gaze dropped to her lips. "One month, *agapi mou*. That's all it will be. One month of being in my bed. Of spending the nights with me deep inside you." His lips twitched, as if he'd made a joke, but his eyes were so dark they seemed bottomless. "I can endure it, if you can."

His words made her blush. How could he joke about the devil's bargain he was forcing on her?

"I hate you," Maria snapped.

Alex grinned. "Hate me all you like, sweet-heart. It's not your heart I'm after."

No, she thought, no, it wasn't. And that was fine because her heart would never be part of this arrangement.

"Understand something, Your Highness," she said, searching for and finding a way to salvage one tiny bit of pride. "Being in your bed is one thing. Participating in what happens there is not something you can ever expect."

His teeth flashed in a quick smile. "A challenge?"

"A statement of fact."

"A challenge," he said flatly. "One I am happy to accept."

He bent his head, brushed his lips over hers. His mouth moved against hers again and again in the lightest of kisses. She wanted to lean into him. Wanted to close her eyes, part her lips, clasp his head and bring it down closer to hers…

I feel nothing, she told herself.

And wished to God it were true.

What in the name of Chronos was she doing? Was she packing everything she owned? Jeans. T-shirts. Sweaters. Sneakers and sandals and, hell, another pair of jeans.

Alex looked at his watch, scowled and shook his wrist. Was the damned thing working? Impossible that only five minutes had passed since she'd first turned on her heel, marched away from him and dragged a suitcase from a corner of the loft.

The loft. Her loft. His lip all but curled. He'd been in Manhattan lofts before. Soaring ceilings. Enormous windows. Brick walls and polished wood floors. Furniture from Scandinavia that made the most of all that open space.

Maria's loft lacked only whatever machines had once been installed here. Raw space, New York realtors called it, and made it sound as if that was a good thing—which, he supposed, it was if you intended to transform it into something habitable.

This was not habitable.

The floor was wood but the finish had long since worn away. The walls were brick. Not warm brick, just brick. Old, dark, depressing. The ceiling soared, all right. It soared straight up to an intimidating tangle of pipes and electrical lines.

As for furniture…there were a couple of work tables. Some cabinets and benches. Boxes. More boxes. And, in this end of the room, farthest from the entry door, a screen that he assumed concealed the bathroom, or what passed for a bathroom, and in front of that, a bed.

Maria's bed.

Neatly made. Simple. Almost convent-like in appearance...

A double bed.

Alex's jaw tightened.

His own bed—his beds, considering the number of homes he owned—his beds were always king-sized. A bachelor's necessity, his brothers called them. Plenty of room for a man and a woman and hours of hot sex.

But a double bed might have advantages.

There'd be little space in which to sprawl while the lovers in Maria's bed took some needed rest. They would have to sleep on their sides, spoon fashion, she with her backside tucked into his groin, her spill of wild, sexy curls tucked beneath his chin. He would wake during the night, feel the heat of her against him and his sex would engorge, fill with heat, throb as he shifted his weight, as she backed up to him, as she awoke and drowsily whispered his name while he sought her moist entrance, while he pistoned within her until she cried out...

Skata!

He was watching Maria pack and turning himself on.

How could she have that much power over him? He didn't like it, not one bit. Men were the ones who held power and if that marked him as old-fashioned, so be it.

He had surely made the right move. Taking her to his bed as often as he wished would purge her from his system. And no matter what she said, she would not be unwilling for long. She could talk about not wanting him all she liked but when he touched her, all that staunch denial fled. To hell with the fact that she despised him. He felt the same about her. What he'd told her was true enough.

Sex had nothing to do with emotion.

As for her threat not to react in his bed... A lie. A magnificent lie. He knew a thousand ways to make her react. His mouth at her breasts. Between her thighs. On her clitoris...

"Damn it," he growled, and strode toward the bed on which her suitcase stood open. "That's enough!"

She swung toward him. "What?"

"Perhaps you have forgotten what my country is like," he said through his teeth. "It is not the wilderness. We have shops."

The understatement of the year, Maria thought. Ellos had all the shops that made Fifth

Avenue paradise and dozens more. Unfortunately, it had the prices to go with them. She wouldn't have the money to step through those doors until she completed this commission. One new outfit, she'd been in debt for life.

Not that that was a possibility. The outfit she'd worn today had pretty much melted her credit card.

"Excuse me," she said with enough sugar in the words to cause diabetic coma, "but I'm not done."

"You are done," he said grimly. "You've packed enough for ten women."

What she'd done was pack enough for one woman who had no idea what the weather was like halfway around the world this time of year. Yes, she could ask him, but that would be a show of weakness. Stupid, perhaps, but that was the way she felt.

So she'd taken jeans. T-shirts. Sandals. Hiking boots. Sweaters. She'd considered something dressy, but what for? She would not be going out in the evenings.

She would be going to the prince's bed.

She stared at him as he closed the suitcase. She hated him as a woman; as an artist, she couldn't help but admire him. Well, no. Not *him*. Not Alexandros Karedes. What she admired was his long, leanly muscled body. His wide shoulders and broad chest. Narrow hips and long legs. The black-as-midnight hair, the dark eyes, the face that Praxiteles might have chiseled from the finest marble.

He was even more beautiful nude.

She remembered that. The corded muscles in his arms. The ridged abs. The powerful thrust of his penis rising from a cluster of dark curls...

Maria swung away and went to the workshop end of the loft.

Forget that. Block it from her mind. Besides, despite all that about the contract, he couldn't mean to enforce such a demand. The more she thought about it, the more assured she grew that the sleep-with-me nonsense was just a particularly nasty way of reminding her that she had no standing in his world.

Fine, she thought, plucking a big leather tote from a shelf and sweeping a handful of tools into it, absolutely fine. Let him play his stupid games. One month, that was all, a month of his bullying tactics and then—

Unless she was wrong.

What if he was serious? What if he really expected her to sleep with him? Well, not 'sleep'. She remembered that one night in his bed. They hadn't slept at all. He'd taken her over and over, driven her out of her mind each time, made her do things…

No. Her breath caught.

He hadn't 'made' her do anything. She'd wanted to do them, things she'd heard of and read about but never, ever imagined she'd want to do.

And would never do again.

Blindly, she grabbed another handful of tools and dumped them in the tote.

What she'd told him was true. If he insisted on holding her to their devil's bargain, she would not participate. She would lie in his bed but she would not move. She'd let his hands seek out every shadowed valley. Let him put his mouth on hers. On her breasts. Between her thighs. She'd let him do everything he wanted but she would not react, she would not, would not…

She gasped as Alex grabbed the tote from her, snapped the lock, then hoisted it and her suitcase from the floor.

"We're leaving."

"I need the rest of those tools—or maybe you thought I work gold and precious stones with tweezers and a crowbar?"

"Did you not hear me when I said you will have the studio of your dreams?"

"I heard you. I still want my own things. It's how people are, when they've worked at the same job for a while. They want the stuff they're familiar with, whether it's a pen or a chisel. I know that's difficult for you to get your head around, considering that you've never had to do a day's work in your life, so you'll just have to take my word for it."

Alex narrowed his eyes. Was that really how she saw him? As a royal dilettante? He thought back to his father's initial reaction when he'd first approached him about bringing new economic life to Aristo.

"What could you possibly bring to Aristo that I have not?" Aegeus said, with his usual imperialistic charm.

A casino, for one. A new commercial port that specialized in handling enormous cargo ships. A colony of upscale second or third or fourth or even fifth homes for multi-billionaires looking for seclusion on the island's northeast coast overlooking the Bay of Apollonia. He had even managed to divert some of the super-rich from building in the new resort town of Jaladhar on the island of Calista, which, together with Aristo, had made up the Kingdom of Adamas until they'd been declared separate nations by his grandfather, King Christos, more than three decades ago.

So, no. Oh, no. He had never worked a day in his life. He travelled between his offices in New York and Ellos, he flew to all the major cities of the world, met and negotiated with hard-headed businessmen and heads of state and it was all nothing but a wealthy man's hobby. Or so this woman thought.

He glared at Maria. At the smug little smile on her lips. Part of him wanted to grab her and shake her.

Part wanted to pull her into his arms and kiss her until she begged for him to do more.

Thank God he wasn't fool enough to do either. Instead, he jerked his chin in her direction.

"Coat," he said briskly. "And shoes. Make it quick or I'll sling you over my shoulder and carry you downstairs just as you are."

He would do it, too.

Maria knew that.

So she pulled on heavy socks, a pair of bulky boots she'd bought the winter she'd almost—almost—decided to try skiing, stuffed her arms through the sleeves of a warm but ugly vintage parka she'd found at the Hell's Kitchen flea market, secured her wild mop of hair with a scrunchy and marched to the door.

Let His Mightiness see what kind of bed-warmer he'd bought himself, she thought grimly.

Useless. He didn't even blink. Instead, he motioned her toward the steps and followed her out of the building. The snow was still coming down but the flakes were big and slow, the kind that normally turned the city into a wonderland.

She could see nothing wonderful about it tonight.

As they stepped off the curb a uniformed driver sprang from behind the wheel of the big limo, touched a finger to his cap and clicked his heels.

Maria snorted.

Alex ignored her.

"Hans," he said.

Hans clicked his heels again. Alex thought about telling him to stop doing that but he'd already told him the same thing at least a dozen times. Apparently, Hans was one of those people who dreamed of the grandeur that was royalty.

Maria, clearly, was not.

Hans reached for the bags. "I'll put them in the trunk," Alex said sharply. "You see to Ms. Santos."

Another click. Maria rolled her eyes. Hans

swept open the rear passenger door, gave her a little bow as she stepped inside the car. The door shut with the sort of solid 'thunk' she figured you expected when a car cost as much as a house. A swirl of warm air, perfumed with the scent of expensive leather, swallowed her up as she fell back into the soft seat.

The only thing that spoiled it was Alex, who opened the other rear door and got in beside her.

"The airport," he said.

The car moved gracefully from the curb. Maria's gut moved, too, but not gracefully. What in the world was she doing? She had to phone Joaquin to say she was leaving, and she certainly had to say goodbye to her mother.

"Wait!"

The car stopped. Alex turned toward her. "Whatever you forgot," he said coldly, "can stay right where it is."

"No. I mean, it can't. I mean..." She took a deep breath. "I can't go with you."

Alex folded his arms. "We've been through all this."

"I can't just leave. I mean...I have to let people know. I have to say goodbye."

"People," he said coldly. "You mean, your 'friend', Joaquin."

She thought of correcting him, but what for? He could believe what he liked.

"And will you tell him the intimate details of our arrangement, *glyka mou*?" he said with a sly smile.

Her head came up. "I will never tell anyone about that."

He stared at her for a long minute. For some insane reason, he wanted to take her in his arms and tell her he would not hurt her, that he would do all he could to bring her pleasure…

To hell with that.

"What's his address?"

"Why?"

"Hans is an excellent driver," Alex said with a tight smile, "but he has one flaw. He can't find a place unless I give him its address."

"Oh," she said quickly, "no, that isn't necessary. Just—Driver? Driver, there's a subway stop two blocks up. If you'd drop me off there—and then I can, ah, I can meet you somewhere later…"

"The address," Alex said quietly, but in a tone so filled with authority that Maria knew she'd lost.

She sank back in her seat.

"One seven four oh Grandview Avenue," she said in a small voice. "That's in the Bronx."

"The Bronx?" the driver said.

"The Bronx," Alex repeated firmly, and the big car started up again.

Alex watched Maria's face as the limo made its way along the snow-laden streets.

She sat huddled in the corner, as far from him as she could get, staring straight ahead, her face pale in the glaring headlights of the few cars coming toward them. The snow had all but emptied the city streets.

She was trembling.

He frowned. Was she cold? Impossible. The sole virtue of that ugly jacket had to be its warmth. Besides, the car's interior was warm.

She was nervous, then. Or anxious. About agreeing to go with him? Not that she'd actually agreed. He'd forced her into it.

Never mind.

Was she nervous about telling her lover she was going away with another man? Alex's jaw tightened. A week from now, hell, a couple of hours from now, her lover would be history. Once they boarded his private plane, he'd take her to the big bedroom in the rear of the cabin, strip her out of that foolish outfit and touch her in ways that would make her forget any man but him.

That was how it had been that night.

Maria, blind with passion. Her skin, silken to the touch. Her mouth drinking from his, her fingers cool against his body, her hands trembling when he clasped them, brought them to his chest, his belly, his erection.

Touch me this way, he'd murmured. *Yes. Like that. Like that.*

She's never done this before, he'd thought in amazement. And then he'd simply stopped thinking, lost in the heat that consumed them.

What a lie!

She'd done everything before. He'd known it as soon as he heard her on the telephone that morning. Until then, she'd had him fooled. And that wasn't easy. He'd been with a lot of women. Too many, he sometimes thought; their faces and names and bodies had become blurred over the years.

Not hers.

Maria's name, her heart-shaped face and its delicate features, her body that was softly curved and not a fashionable arrangement of hard bones and flesh, even her voice…

He had forgotten nothing. She came to him in his dreams, telling him she wanted him.

Turning yourself on again, you idiot? he

thought angrily as he shifted in the deep leather seat.

Well, there'd be no more of that.

He knew what this was all about, if he was honest. Ego? Maybe a little. Anger? Okay, that, too. Payback? Absolutely. But the real reason he wanted her was much more basic.

The hair of the dog that bit you. Driving out demons. Whatever you wanted to call it. Have enough sex with Maria Santos and he'd wipe her name, her face, everything about her from his mind.

A month from now, he'd be happy to see the last of her. Whether she was clever in bed or not, he'd never come across a woman who could hold his interest for much longer than that. This one would be no exception, not even if she went from waif to temptress, fire to ice…

"It's the building right over there."

Her voice was low. Alex blinked and realized the car had slowed to a crawl. He looked out the window and saw a nondescript street, cars packed tightly along the curb, and a looming wall of apartment buildings.

"This one, miss?" Hans asked.

"*Sí.* Yes."

It was the first time she'd lapsed into Spanish

since the phone call—and since she'd cursed him. She sounded breathless. Stressed. His jaw tightened. Was she nervous about visiting her lover and telling him her plans?

If he'd been her lover, she'd have had the right to be terrified. He could not imagine agreeing to her going off with another man for a month. Not for a day. Not if she belonged to him.

The limo eased into the space beside a fire hydrant. The driver turned off the engine and reached for the door handle.

"Thank you," Maria said quickly, "but that isn't necessary. I can open the door my—"

"Stay in the car, Hans." Alex's voice was cold. "I'll take care of Ms. Santos."

A blast of frigid air swept in as he opened the door. Maria's heart skipped a beat. Did the Prince of Arrogance think he was going inside with her? Not in a million years.

"Thank you," she said, forcing a polite smile, "but I can manage."

"Don't be silly, *glyka mou*. It's late, the street is nearly deserted. What kind of gentleman would permit a woman to be alone under such conditions?"

His tone had gone from harsh to silken. A spider's web was silken, too. She didn't want him with her, not only because then he would know she hadn't come to see Joaquin but because he would know too much.

"Maria. I'm waiting."

He was leaning into the car, his patrician face rigid. Anger swept through her. Did he think he could take over every aspect of her life?

"Keep waiting, then. I don't require your assistance. And let me assure you, Your Highness, if you think you are a gentleman—"

She gasped as he caught her shoulders and pulled her from the car.

"You will not talk to me that way," he growled. "I don't give a damn what you do or do not require. What matters is what *I* require. For the next month, you'll do things my way or not at all. Is that clear?"

"Yessir," she said, and touched her stiff fingers to her forehead. "Of course, sir," she added, and clicked her heels. Then she jerked her chin up, stepped around him and marched over the snowy sidewalk to the building's entry.

Alex could feel his face burning.

He shot a furious glare at Hans, sitting straight as a ramrod behind the wheel. He gave no sign that he'd seen or heard what had just happened.

Alex took a deep breath. Then he trudged after

Maria through the snow. Her feet, in those hideous boots, moved up and down without interference but he was wearing leather mocs— handmade leather mocs, he thought grimly, and they were already cold and sodden.

Great. He was about to come face to face with the man who'd been her lover and his damned shoes would probably fall off his feet when he…

Panagia mou!

What kind of place was this for a love nest? The entrance door had a broken lock. The lobby smelled of mice and mildew. What remained of a mural clung pathetically to a graffiti-scarred wall. There was an elevator but Maria ignored it and headed for the stairs.

"Four flights," she said briskly, without looking back at him. "Are you up to that, Your Highness?"

He didn't bother replying, he simply climbed the steps behind her. One flight. Two. Three. At last, they reached the fifth-floor landing.

"This is where he lives?"

Alex sounded incredulous. She hated him for that, and for forcing himself into this part of her life.

"Answer me!" He clasped her wrist and spun her toward him. "Your lover expects you to come to him in a dump like this?"

The door to the apartment directly ahead swung open. Alex looked up, angry at himself, at Maria, at the unwanted intrusion.

"What the hell do you want?" he snarled at the shadowy figure in the doorway.

The figure stepped forward into the dim light of the stairwell landing. It was a woman. Small. Dark-haired. Wrapped in a wool bathrobe.

"Maria?"

Maria took a deep breath. "*Sí*, Mama. It's me."

CHAPTER FIVE

IT'S ME, Mama, Maria said.

And then no one said anything.

For an eternity? For a few seconds? Alex couldn't be sure. The only certainty was that he'd made one hell of a mistaken assumption.

And he'd mortified Maria. The proof was in the rigidity of her posture, the angle of her head. This place, this depressing setting, this woman making absolutely no move toward her daughter, were not things she'd wanted him to see.

So what? he asked himself coldly. Wasn't it his intention to humiliate Maria Santos? This was just one more way to do it.

But even as he thought that he found himself moving closer to her, putting his hand lightly on her shoulder in a gesture of unspoken support.

The woman in the doorway spoke first. Her words were not those of a loving mother, delighted to see her child. They were, instead, accusatory.

"Do you have any idea how late it is, Maria? I was on my way to bed."

He saw the color rise in Maria's face. His hand tightened on her shoulder.

"I'm sorry, Mama. I should have phoned first—"

"And who is this with you? Why have you brought a man to my home?"

"Forgive me, Mrs. Santos," Alex said pleasantly. He gave Maria what he hoped was a reassuring smile, then stepped forward. "It's my fault, entirely. I'm afraid I was in such a hurry to get things done that the lateness of the hour never occurred to me."

"And you are…?"

"I am Alexandros Karedes. Prince Alexandros Karedes."

The Santos woman's eyebrows rose.

"Prince?"

"From the kingdom of Aristo. Perhaps you've heard of it," he said politely, knowing she would have. You could not read a magazine or see a television program about the rich and famous without hearing of places like Dubai, Monaco and Aristo.

"And you know my daughter?"

"Indeed. In fact, Maria and I are going to be spending the next few weeks together."

Maria gave him a look that should have turned him to stone. "The prince means we'll be working together."

"Maria is making my mother's birthday gift."

Luz raised her dark eyebrows. "Maria? Is this what you meant when I called you a little while ago?"

Alex looked at Maria. She glared even as color rose in her cheeks. It had been her mother on the phone, not her lover. Why did that please him? Whether she had a lover or not didn't matter. She would be his for the next four weeks. Who gave a damn if she came home to Joaquin when the month ended?

"*Sí*, Mama, it was."

He could almost see Luz mulling that over. Finally, she stepped aside and motioned them forward. "Come inside. I don't want to bother the neighbors."

Maria looked like a wild animal who wanted to escape a trap, but she jerked her head in assent and moved past him into the apartment.

The entry foyer was big; it led down two steps into a living room that must have been elegant in its day but now was dimly lit and depressing.

Luz made no offer of coffee or tea; she took a chair and when Maria hovered uncertainly, Alex took her elbow. He felt her stiffen, knew she wanted to jerk free but she let him draw her down beside him on a small, sagging, blanket-covered sofa.

"You see," Alex said pleasantly, "my mother—"

"She is the queen?"

"Queen Tia. Yes. Her sixtieth birthday is next month, and—"

He launched into an explanation of the planned celebration. The state dinner in the palace. The ball that would follow. The presentation of Maria's necklace to the queen at precisely midnight, followed by fireworks. The fact that Maria was accompanying him to Aristo so she could consult personally with the queen and with him, should questions arise about the design of the piece.

"You mean, my daughter will leave New York?"

"Yes," Alex said politely, "but I can assure you—"

"Well, if it doesn't worry her to leave me all alone, who am I to complain? I am not well, Your Highness. Perhaps Maria has mentioned it."

"You're fine, Mama. Your doctors say—"

"What do doctors know?" Luz crossed herself. "We can only pray for the best. Besides, I suppose you're determined to live out this fantasy of yours."

Alex could see a vein throb in Maria's temple.

"Could we please have this discussion another time?" she said, but Luz ignored her.

"Do you have children, Prince Alexandros?"

"I'm not married, Mrs. Santos," Alex said politely, though being polite was growing difficult.

"Well, when you do, you'll understand that a mother's sole concern is for her child's welfare. Maria's cousin, Angela—"

"I'm sure the prince isn't interested in Angela."

"Angela is a wonderful girl. She has an excellent position with an insurance company. She's offered many, many times to arrange for Maria to have an interview there. Why, only this evening, I told Maria of Angela's promotion. She'll be earning thirty thousand dollars a year!" Luz leaned toward her daughter. "And I didn't get the chance to tell you the rest. Angela's engaged. To her supervisor, can you imagine? She has done so well for herself. It's hard to believe you and she graduated high school at the same time."

The sofa was small. Maria's thigh was against

his. Alex could feel her trembling. With anger? With despair? Not that it mattered to him…

"We had different goals," Maria said carefully. "Angela went straight to work. I went to college."

"And quit."

"I didn't quit, I changed schools. I went to the Fashion Institute of Technology." A touch of pride edged her words. "It was not easy to get in."

Luz made a face. "Such foolishness! Two years spent studying what? Drawing? Making geegaws? And meanwhile, your cousin, Angela, was—"

The hell with this, Alex thought, and he clasped Maria's hand. She tried to tug it away but he threaded his fingers through hers.

"Maria," he said smoothly, "I think it's time we told your mother the truth."

Her eyes went dark and wild. "Alex. Alex, please—"

"I admire your modesty, *glyka mou,*" he said softly, "but surely your mother should know the details—of this commission."

Maria let out a breath. Luz shrugged her shoulders.

"I know them already, Prince Alexandros. My daughter entered a contest and lost. She's won it now because the real winner backed out."

"You make it sound as if Maria entered a sweepstakes, Mrs. Santos," Alex said with a smile that barely softened the tightly spoken words. "In fact, fifty of the world's most prestigious jewelry designers submitted sketches for my father's perusal. He and his ministers narrowed the field to three but the final selection was the king's." He paused. "He chose an excellent entry—but from the start, Maria's design was the queen's choice."

Maria's eyes lit. "Was it?" she said softly.

Alex nodded. What was the harm in telling her the truth?

"The necklace your daughter creates will be photographed by every major magazine. It will be featured on television news on virtually every continent. And when the queen's birthday celebration ends, it will be displayed alongside the Crowns of Aristo and Adamas, two of the most famous royal crowns in the world."

Luz seemed to take it all in. Then she nodded and looked at Maria.

"This is a fine opportunity, *mia hija*."

"*Sí*, Mama. I know it is."

"You must not squander it. Such good fortune may not come your way again."

Alex glanced at Maria. She had a stiff smile

pinned to her lips. He couldn't blame her. Not that her feelings meant anything to him, but couldn't her mother work up a little enthusiasm? His own mother had always been loving. Not the way mothers were loving in the books he'd read when he was growing up, or even in the ways he'd observed when he spent an occasional holiday weekend with a friend from boarding school.

Tia had not tousled his hair or kissed his scraped knees; she had not tucked him in at night or sat with him at breakfast in the morning. He'd longed for those things as a kid but he'd understood. She was the queen. His father was the king. His parents had grave responsibilities; from his earliest years on, he'd been groomed to respect that.

But Tia had applauded his every academic achievement and sports trophy. Even Aegeus, who had always treated his children, especially his sons, with cool removal, would have offered a word of praise at news as important as this.

"This was more than good fortune," he said coolly. Maria looked at him in surprise. Hell, he'd surprised himself. "Your daughter's talent is the reason she won the commission."

Maria's counterfeit smile had given way to one that was soft and sweet. He wanted to cup her face with his hand, taste that sweetness, kiss her not as he had before but gently, tenderly…

A muscle knotted in his jaw.

"It's time we left," he said brusquely, and rose to his feet.

It had stopped snowing; the street was clear and a plow truck disappearing just ahead, red lights blinking, was the reason.

Hans popped from the driver's seat of the big limo and swept the rear door open. Maria stepped in; Alex followed her.

"Where to, sir?"

What was that sound? Was Maria—was she crying?

"Sir? To the airport?"

Alex forced his attention to his driver, then dug his BlackBerry from his pocket. There was one text message. It was from his pilot and it was brief and to the point.

"Runways are open. Flight plan has been filed."

"The airport," he said briskly, and settled back in the seat.

The big car moved swiftly through the streets. Maria said nothing; her face was turned to the window. If she'd been weeping, she seemed to have stopped.

Alex cleared his throat.

"I forgot to leave my phone number for your mother. I'll have my secretary call her with it first thing tomorrow. Is there anyone else you wish to notify?"

She shook her head.

"Not even—" He paused. *Don't,* he told himself, but the need to say it was the same as the need to touch an aching tooth, even though you knew it was a mistake. "Not even your *friend*, Joaquin?"

She swung toward him. "He *is* my friend," she said fiercely, "despite what you think. And I have my own cell phone, thank you very much. I don't need you or your secretary to do it for me."

"You needn't bite my head off. I just—I just wondered if, perhaps—"

"Look, you did one decent thing tonight, Your Highness. You—you tried to defend me to my mother. I suppose I owe you my thanks for that. Just don't—don't spoil it."

"I didn't defend you. I spoke the truth. My mother loved your design." He hesitated. "Frankly, I agreed with her that it was the best. Why should that be a secret?"

She lifted her chin and looked directly at him. They had just pulled up to a traffic light. The red glow lit her lovely face with color and yes, she had been crying. The delicate skin under her eyes was swollen.

"If it isn't a secret, why didn't you tell me right away?"

Alex felt a quick stab of guilt, but why should he? Maria had not been honest with him, and her lie of omission had been far greater than his.

"I told you what you needed to know," he said coldly. "There was no reason to tell you anything more."

She gave a little laugh. "Such diplomatic words, Alexandros. Why, if I didn't know better, I'd think you were a—" Her face turned white.

"Maria?"

"Tell the driver to pull over."

"What is it?"

"I'm going to be—"

Alex lowered the privacy screen and jerked his thumb toward the curb. Hans steered to it and pulled up, Alex threw his door open and Maria shot past him. He was right on her heels; he caught her by the shoulders as she bent over and was viciously ill.

"Go away," she gasped. "I don't want you to—"

Another spasm shook her. He could feel the violence of it and his hands clasped her more tightly. When she was done, she stood straight, her back still to him, her body racked with tremors.

"Maria," he said softly. "Are you okay?"

She nodded. "I'm fine."

She wasn't. Her voice was thready and the trembling had increased. Alex cursed and turned her toward him. She stood with her head down.

"What happened?"

"I don't know. Flu, I think. Everyone has it."

God, she looked so fragile. Not silly, lost in that enormous and ugly jacket, but terribly, heartbreakingly delicate.

He dug a handkerchief from his pocket and held it toward her. She shook her head.

"Not your handkerchief. I'll soil it."

"Damn it, Maria," he said, and put his hand under her chin, lifted her face and dabbed her lips carefully with the snowy-white linen.

She was still shaking.

Alex lifted her in his arms. "No," she said, but he ignored her, ducked his head, carried her inside the car, settled her close against him and pressed the intercom button.

Hans answered immediately. "Sir?"

"Turn up the heat," Alex said crisply. "And take us to the nearest hospital.

"No," Maria said, even more emphatically. "I don't want to go to a hospital."

"You need a doctor."

"For heaven's sake, I was sick. Sick, that's all. Flu. Or maybe something I ate."

"You look like you don't eat enough," Alex said, more sharply than he'd intended but it was true. Holding her in his arms, he'd realized she was as light as the proverbial feather.

"I am fine. I don't need to be coddled."

Yes, he thought, she did—but he knew that edge in her voice by now, just as he knew the proud angle of her head.

"Okay. Great. No coddling. Hans?"

"Sir?"

"The airport."

The intercom light blinked off. Maria stared straight ahead, wrapped in mortification. Of all things to happen. To get sick in front of this man. To have him insist on staying with her. To have him wipe her face and now to be sitting within the circle of his arm...

"I am perfectly capable of sitting on my own," she said coolly.

He let her move away. From the corner of her

eye, she could see him opening a mahogany compartment built into the side of the car. Taking something from it. A bottle of water. A big white linen napkin.

"Look at me," he said as he poured the water on the napkin.

She looked. Their eyes met. What was in his? Pity? Damn it, she didn't want his pity. She didn't want anything from him.

Carefully, he began to wash her face. She jerked back. He sighed, cupped the back of her head and went right on washing.

It felt wonderful.

When he was done, she gave him a jerky nod. "Thank you," she said stiffly and turned away but, once again, she could see what he was doing from the corner of her eye. Putting the water and napkin back in the compartment. Taking out another bottle, this one filled with an amber liquid. Taking out a crystal tumbler. Opening the bottle, pouring the liquid into the glass…

"Drink this."

She swung toward him. Bad idea. Everything began to spin. The interior of the car, Alex's face. The glass he was holding toward her.

"Damn it," he said, reaching for her, "you're as white as a sheet."

"I'm—I'm okay. I'm not going to be sick again. I'm just a little woozy…"

Alex's arms swept around her. "Don't," she said, but she was speaking into the hard wall of his chest as he lifted her into his lap.

He was warm. Strong. He smelled of snow and cold and of the clean male scent she remembered, had never forgotten.

"Let go of me," she said, and hated how her voice shook but the truth was, she felt awful. Not sick to her stomach anymore, just cold and shaky and awful.

"Stop arguing with everything I say and drink this."

His tone was gruff but he held her with care. Well, of course. He certainly didn't want to risk having her throw up all over his magnificent automobile.

The glass was at her mouth.

"What is it?"

"Poison," he said, but when she looked up at him, he was smiling. "It's brandy."

"I don't—"

"Yes. I know. You don't need brandy. Well, I do." He took a drink from the glass, then brought it to her lips again. "For once, just do as I ask without giving me a tough time, okay?"

The brandy smelled wonderful. She thought of how it would feel, warm and soothing, and of how his mouth had touched the rim of the glass…

It was safer to think about doing as he'd commanded.

She did, and knew she'd been right. The brandy was warm and comforting. So was the man who held her. The thought, unbidden, unexpected, set her heart racing and she pushed the glass away.

"That's enough. And you can let go of me. I'm perfectly fine."

He answered by gathering her closer. "It's late," he said brusquely. "And I've had a long day. I think you have, too. So stop fighting me, Maria. You're cold and shaky and I'm not at all convinced you don't need a doctor."

"I already said I didn't."

"Then do as you're told. Finish the brandy, put your head against my shoulder and maybe, just maybe, I'll believe you."

"You're a—a martinet," she said bitterly. "Did anyone ever tell you that?"

It was such an old-fashioned word that it made him laugh.

"I've been called a lot of things by a lot of women, *glyka mou*, but that is a first." He sank back in the seat; she had no choice but to sink back with him. "Now close your eyes and rest. We'll be at the airport soon."

Rest? She'd won a competition that had been the goal of the world's best jewelry designers— and handed her life over to one of the world's most gorgeous, sexiest men. How could she possibly rest? Surely, the man holding her had his choice of women, a different one every night if he wished, and yet he wanted her…

Her lashes drooped.

She couldn't rest. Or sleep. Or…

Maria sighed, burrowed closer against him, and tumbled into sleep.

Alex felt the tension leave her. He looked down, saw the dark shadow of her lashes against the sculpted curve of her cheek.

The woman was impossible. Argumentative. Prickly. Sharp-tongued.

She was also beautiful and fragile and…

And, he reminded himself, she was a manipulative liar. The sooner he had her in his bed, the better. She would not spin lies to him there; he would not permit it. He would make love to her until she sobbed his name, until her need for him was real, and that would happen as soon as he had her, alone, on his plane.

But when they reached it, he carried a still-sleeping Maria through the big cabin, to the privacy of his bedroom. Sat her on the edge of the bed. Took off her jacket and her boots. Took off his jacket and soggy shoes, as well.

Her eyelids fluttered but did not lift. "Alexandros?" she murmured.

She had called him that the night they'd made love. That was the only name he'd given her, just 'Alexandros'. "Alex, if you prefer," he'd added, but not the rest.

Not that she'd needed it, he thought grimly. She had known his identity; she had targeted him.

"Wake up," he said coldly as he lay her back against the pillows. She didn't. He looked at her again. Even in sleep, she looked exhausted. And incredibly lovely.

He lay down next to her. Drew the cashmere throw from the foot of the bed over them both. Maria sighed in her sleep and turned toward him. What else could he do except gather her into his arms?

CHAPTER SIX

MARIA awoke in total confusion.

Her heart thumped with terror. *Where was she?*

Everything about this room was wrong. The bed. The faint light stealing in through the window. Even the feel of the silk bed linen under her cheek, the whisper-weight of the blanket...

The pillow beside hers. Indented, as if someone's head had rested on it. A faint scent. Clean. Crisp. Male.

"Ohmygod," she whispered, and shot up against the pillows. A bad move. Her stomach did a slow roll. She bolted from the bed, looked around wildly, saw the bathroom and barely got there in time.

She retched until the muscles of her diaphragm ached. Shaken and shaking, she closed her eyes and sank down on the cold tile floor.

Easy, she told herself, *just take it easy.*

Seconds later, she stood, washed her face, unscrewed the top from a small bottle of mouthwash and rinsed her mouth until the bottle was empty.

Boneless, on legs that seemed to be made of over-cooked pasta, she sank down on the closed commode.

She remembered it all. Alex's arrival. The royal commission. The awful visit to Luz, the humiliation of being sick afterward…

Most of all, the unbelievable proposition Alex had made—and she had accepted.

Was this a hotel room? As if in answer, the floor seemed to give a gentle dip. Not a hotel room. This was his plane. They were somewhere over the ocean and she couldn't even remember getting on board. Her memory took her as far as being sick in the snow. Alex cradling her in his arms. The warming swallows of brandy.

Maria groaned and buried her face in her hands.

Had she slept with him? No. Heat flooded her body. Definitely, no. If Alex had made love to her— Correction. If they'd had sex, she'd remember. Besides, except for her jacket and boots, she was still dressed in the ratty outfit she'd worn last night.

Somehow, the thought that she'd slept between silk sheets and beneath what was probably a cashmere blanket dressed like this made her want to laugh.

God, she was coming apart! Aches where she'd never had aches. Laughter that could just as easily turn to tears. Nausea when she least expected it. Joaquin was right. She'd been working too hard. Stress could do terrible things.

She rose to her feet. There was a stall shower. A big terrycloth robe hanging from a hook. Shampoo and soap and—

And Alex, just outside the bedroom door.

How was she going to face him? What was she going to say? Could she ask him if he'd slept with her? Well, not with her. In the same bed. Not that it mattered. He had the right. Hadn't she agreed to share his bed, and not just for sleep?

It was a miracle he hadn't held her to that unspoken agreement already, but then a woman who tossed her cookies at a man's feet wasn't exactly a turn-on. Not that she wanted to turn him on. Not that she wanted him to undress her, touch her, carry her to his bed and do more, much more than sleep next to her...

Someone knocked at the door. The knob rattled. Maria swung around and stared as if it were a live thing about to launch an attack.

"Ms. Santos?" A woman's voice. "Ms. Santos?"

She took a deep breath. "Yes?"

The door opened. A pleasant-faced woman of about fifty smiled at her.

"Good morning, Ms. Santos. I'm Thalia. The stewardess. The prince asked me to tell you we'll be landing in a couple of hours. He asks that you join him for breakfast."

Maria felt her face heat. "Thank you."

"I've left your bag at the foot of the bed."

Could her cheeks get any hotter? "Fine. Thank you again."

Thalia smiled, stepped out of the room and shut the door behind her. Maria flew to it and turned the lock.

How could she face anyone? She'd all but died of humiliation just now and there were other people to deal with. The pilot. A co-pilot. Half the kingdom of Aristo, for all she knew. *So what?* the logical part of her said. Common sense assured her that Prince Alexandros had a long tradition of having women travel with him and share his bed.

The knowledge would come as no shock to anyone.

Yes, but it came as a shock to her. She had never been a mistress before.

The fact was, she had never been with a man

before that night two months ago. Not that His Royal Arrogance would believe it if she told him. Not that she *would* tell him. Her humiliation was already devastating enough. Why make it worse? Far better to let him think that she was as experienced as he obviously believed.

Why hadn't she thought of that sooner?

Maria stripped off her clothes and stepped into the shower.

Alex had called her a liar. She wasn't, but she could carry things off when she had to. Hadn't she prepped for the interview at FIT without letting her mother know? And then there'd been the interview itself, when she'd sat in a waiting room like an ugly duckling lost in a bevy of swans. And years later, after she'd won the Caligari prize and approached a buyer at a posh Fifth Avenue store with a small box filled with earrings of her own design...

Oh yes, she thought as she tilted her face up to the spray, yes, she could do this. Pretend that being his sex toy for a month meant nothing. Not a problem.

Not at all.

Where in blazes was Maria?

Alex had awakened hours ago. Awakened?

His mouth twisted. He had not really slept. How could a man sleep with a woman curled against him, her breath warm and light against his throat, her hand on his chest? Maria had curved her body into his as if she'd belonged there. He'd told himself it didn't affect him and it hadn't...

For about thirty seconds.

Then, he'd gone into a full state of arousal.

He'd imagined rolling her onto her back. Undressing her. Caressing her. Imagined her waking slowly as she felt his hands and mouth moving gently on her flesh.

"Alexandros?" she'd have whispered, as she had that night they'd spent together, as she had just a little while ago, when he'd put her to bed, and he'd have said, *Yes, it's Alexandros. Say my name again, Maria. Touch me with your cool hands. Open your mouth so I can taste your sweetness...*

That was when he'd shot from the bed.

A cold shower. A change of clothes. Then he'd left the room without a backward glance because he hadn't trusted himself. He'd waited weeks for this. He wasn't going to take her now, when she was exhausted and sick and only half aware of him.

He wanted her wide awake when he possessed

her, wanted her eyes on his as he took what she had only pretended to give him that first time.

His flight crew, of course, had asked no questions, nor had Thalia when he'd told her to inform his guest that they'd be landing soon.

"Is Ms. Santos awake?" he'd asked brusquely, when Thalia brought him coffee.

"Yessir. I gave her your message."

Alex looked at his watch. Fifteen minutes had gone by. What was taking her so long? Did she think she could stay locked in the bedroom? That she could put off what would happen next?

The hell she could.

They'd land soon, his car would be waiting. He would drive to his apartment in Ellos and take her to his bed.

He looked at his watch again. He was weary of playing her games. He put down his coffee cup. Blotted his lips with a linen napkin. There was still time to assert his possession now…

The door at the rear of the cabin opened. Maria stood framed within it; her eyes met his. He saw her take a breath and then she started toward him. The ugly sweats and boots had been replaced by a pale gray long-sleeved sweater that fell to her hips, black tights and pale gray ankle boots. Her hair, still damp, tumbled around her shoulders.

His gut tightened. By God, she was beautiful. And composed.

He had not expected that. The fact was, he wasn't sure what he'd expected. Tears, maybe. Pleas that he send her home. He'd judged wrong. The look on her face was a study in self-assurance.

"Good morning," he said, and rose to his feet. He gestured to the chair opposite his. She took it, plucked the napkin from under the heavy silverware and spread it in her lap. "How do you feel?"

"I'm fine. I'm sorry about last night—"

"That you slept curled in my arms?"

"That I got sick," she said quickly, but the tiniest bit of color crept into her face.

So. Perhaps she wasn't as self-confident as she appeared.

"I'm just happy a night's sleep helped. I tried not to disturb you when I left the bed," he said, pouring coffee for her. He glanced at her, to see what effect his deliberate use of the word 'bed' had made. None. None at all. Her expression was impersonal again. "You were curled so tightly in my arms that I had to disentangle us."

There it was again. That little rush of color. She shot him a look, then buried it in a sip of coffee. She swallowed, looked up. The tip of her tongue peeped out; she swiped it over her lips. To his annoyance, he felt his body stir.

"I was sure I'd wake you when I took my arm out from around your shoulders."

She looked straight at him. "I thought your stewardess said we'd be landing soon."

"A change of subject, *agapimeni*?" His tone was pure silk. "Did you want to discuss something other than the fact that you slept with me last night?"

"We shared the same bed," she said, looking him straight in the eye. "I'm sure you know the difference between that and what people mean when they say they slept together." Her lips compressed. "Besides, I didn't know I rated a change of subject. I thought mistresses were expected to comply with the wishes of their masters. That is what I will be, isn't it? Your mistress? I mean, isn't that what one calls a woman who warms a man's bed?"

Damn it! *He* was the one who could feel his face filling with heat. What a hell of a little speech, and had she deliberately waited until Thalia was in earshot? His stewardess had been with him for years; if asked, he'd have said nothing could rattle her but hadn't her eyebrows just taken a surprised lift?

Alex tossed his napkin on the table and got to his feet. Two could play at this game of control—but only one would be the winner.

"We'll be on the ground soon," he said coldly. "And then there'll be plenty of time for me to make my wishes clear—and for you to make absolutely certain you comply with them."

The last time Maria had come to Aristo, the only time, had been in early December, the start of the Mediterranean winter.

The plane had taxied to a jet way; she'd disembarked along with scores of other travel-weary coach passengers and sleepwalked through the terminal to a luggage carousel where she'd waited for her suitcase to thump its way toward her. Then she'd headed outside and waited in line for a taxi.

Arriving in the kingdom with a prince of the Royal House of Karedes was very different.

Alex's jet landed and taxied to an area far from the busy terminal. Two men wheeled a staircase to the door. The captain and co-pilot left the cockpit and saluted as she and Alex moved past them; Thalia dropped a little curtsy to Alex and smiled at her.

"Enjoy your stay, miss."

Alex slid his arm around her waist. "I'll see to it Ms. Santos enjoys every minute."

Was she the only one who heard the ironic undertone in his words? She couldn't tell; Thalia's face showed nothing but Maria felt a tinge of heat wash into hers.

No, she told herself fiercely, *no!* She would not let him take control again. Determinedly, she shrugged free of his encircling arm and went down the stairs.

In December, the Aristan skies had been a brilliant blue and the day unseasonably warm. Now, in early February, the air held a distinct chill. Just as chilling was the sight of the uniformed chauffeur standing at attention beside a black limousine even more imposing than the one that had ferried them around New York.

A shudder went through her, and Alex immediately took off his leather jacket and wrapped it around her shoulders.

"I don't need that," she said, trying to shrug it away, but he clasped the collar, brought the edges together and, in doing so, drew her closer.

"But you do, *agapimeni,*" he said, smiling though the smile never reached his eyes. "Besides, didn't you just tell me the first rule a mistress must follow is compliance?"

"Don't count your chickens before they hatch," Maria said coolly. "I'm not your mistress yet."

His eyes grew darker than midnight.

"You will be, *glyka mou*," he said huskily. "And very soon."

He brushed a strand of hair from her cheek and hooked it behind her ear. His gaze fell to her lips. Was he going to kiss her, despite the people watching from the top of the stairs and the chauffeur waiting beside the car?

If he did—if he did, she would stand straight and still within his arms and give him nothing in return.

"Did you hear what I said, Maria? An hour from now, you'll be in my bed."

Her pulse rocketed. It took all her strength to respond with what she hoped was a cool smile.

"Thank you for the warning, Your Highness. It's always helpful to be prepared for something unpleasant."

To her amazement, Alex laughed.

"Very nicely done." His hands swept into her hair and he tilted her face to his. "But a sad little lie." His smile faded. "Tell me how unpleasant it is after I have you undressed," he whispered. "Say it when my mouth is at your breast, when it is between your thighs. Tell me then, *glyka mou*, and I might just believe you."

She felt her nipples peak, felt the swift rush of desire spear low in her belly. He seemed to know what effect his words had because he bent his head and gave her a quick, possessive kiss.

"Get in the car, *agapi mou*," he said, and the look of satisfaction on his hard, beautiful face made her wonder who she hated the most, Alex or herself.

The car moved swiftly through the streets of Ellos.

Alex was on his cell phone, talking softly as buildings flashed by. She recognized the small hotel she'd stayed at, the busy street where she'd first met him. The romantic restaurant he'd taken her to, the little park where he'd kissed her.

He'd told the truth, she thought, and drew a shaky breath. He'd have her in his bed very soon. His apartment was only a couple of blocks away.

But the car didn't take the turn that would have brought them there.

Where was he taking her, then?

She threw him a glance. He'd put the phone away; he sat with his arms folded over his chest, looking distant and formidable, and she decided she'd sooner die than ask. Besides, what did it matter? Maybe he had rules for this kind of thing. Or maybe he didn't want her in his apartment. Maybe there was another woman there already. Or maybe he preferred to keep his women in a hotel.

The limo swooped up a ramp and onto a highway. A sign in both Greek and English flashed by.

To the North Coast Beaches and the Bay of Apollonia.

Beaches? Bays? She was a city girl. Streets, noise, traffic were her natural habitat. Beaches and bays sounded foreign. Isolated.

"Aren't we going to your apartment?"

She spoke without thinking, regretted it almost immediately, but Alex had a ready reply.

"We were, but I changed my mind. I'm taking you to a place where your compliance will be assured."

Her heart skipped a beat. She thought of telling him he wasn't funny but that would be a sign of surrender, and the last thing this man would have from her was surrender.

Her refusal to bend to his will was all she had left, and she was intent on keeping it.

The drive took what seemed a very long time.

They had reached the bay; the sign at the exit said so but the proof was in the spectacular view from a road that now hugged high, curving cliffs above sand so white it looked as if it were made of crushed pearls. Beyond that stretched a sea of deep, brilliant blue, so beautiful it took her breath away.

All right. She had to break her self-imposed silence.

"Is that the Bay of Apollonia?"

Alex nodded. "Named for the god, Apollo. Legend says that Virgil wrote a poem about this place some two thousand years ago."

"Virgil? But he was Roman."

"Aristo and its sister island, Calista, were first part of the Greek Empire and then were ruled by Rome. You're familiar with Virgil?"

Maria stiffened. "I might not have had your tutors and private schools, Alexandros, but the New York City schools provided me with an excellent education."

"I didn't mean to imply…"

"Yes. You did. You don't know a thing about me but you have no trouble jumping to all kinds of conclusions."

"I might say the same of you, *glyka mou*."

Maria looked at him. "You mean," she said sweetly, "you didn't have tutors? You didn't go to private schools?"

"Well, no. I mean, I did—but I have to admit, I tuned out most of what I learned in Latin III, which was pretty much when we dealt with Virgil. I guess I'm just surprised you didn't do the same."

He grinned, and it instantly transformed him from cold despot to the gorgeous, easygoing man she'd met that night two months ago. She didn't want that. Didn't want to remember that night, how he'd made her feel when he'd made love to her.

"Anyway, yes, Virgil wrote about the Bay of Apollonia. He called it an ambrosial sea of sapphire."

How could she not reply to that? Maria sighed and gazed out at the bay again.

"He was right," she said softly, "though I've never seen a sapphire that magnificent. But if I did—"

"If you did?"

"I'd use it as the center stone in a ring. I'd make the setting of twenty-four-karat gold to suggest the brilliance of the sun, and mount the sapphire between a pair of small, perfect diamonds to represent the sister islands of Aristo and Calista."

"They're not that anymore," Alex said, a bit

grimly. "The unified kingdom of Adamas is just a memory until, if and when the islands are somehow reunited."

"Is that what people hope will happen?"

"It's what King Christos hoped would happen when he gave dominion of one island to his daughter, Anya, and the other to my father, Aegeus."

"Was that when Christos had the Stefani diamond split in two?"

Alex raised an eyebrow. "You've done your homework."

"Did you think I designed the necklace for your mother out of nothing? Of course I did my homework. I know the diamond was the biggest pink diamond ever mined on Calista, that it dates to the time of Richard the Lionheart and that it was the center of the crown of Adamas until it was cut in half in ninety seventy-four." Maria flushed. "I don't know why I'm telling you all this when you already know it."

The lady was full of surprise, Alex thought, watching her in silence for a little while. Then he cleared his throat.

"What will you do with the money from the commission?"

"What will I do with it?" Her disbelieving tone suggested he'd lost his mind.

"Yes. Surely, it's enough to buy the perfect sapphire, the perfect diamonds—"

"You mean, it's enough to put a down payment on my loft. Buy some new equipment. Pay some overdue bills. Pay some bills for my mother, maybe even convince her to move to a nicer place." She gave a rueful laugh. "That's what I'll do with the commission."

"You support your mother?"

Maria gave a little shrug. "She isn't up to working."

"Surely, she could—"

"She doesn't think so. And I owe her. She sacrificed everything for me…"

"You can't really believe that," he said, a touch of anger in his words.

"What does it matter? I do what must be done, Your Highness, the same as most people, but what would you know about that, in your world?"

"That's unfair."

"Is it?" Her lips stretched in a smile. "You show up at my door. You give me the most wonderful news imaginable."

"And that's bad?"

"Then you tell me the only way this—this

miracle will happen is if I agree to sleep with you."

His eyes narrowed. "Trying to get out of our deal, Maria?" He moved quickly, covered the distance between them and caught her by the elbows. "All I did was turn the tables," he said in a low voice. "You sct the trap the first time. Now it's my turn."

Maria could feel the sting of angry tears. She didn't want to cry in front of him!

"Let go of me."

"Why? Because you don't like the truth?"

"You wouldn't know the truth if it bit you! There was no trap! You seduced me."

"I seduced you the way a chicken seduces a fox! You were good, I have to admit. I really believed you were a shy Miss Innocent lost on the streets of a strange city."

"Bastardo!" Maria hissed.

Alex slid his hands to her wrists, clamped them hard and dragged her toward him.

"You knew who I was. You intended to use me." His eyes narrowed. "Now I'm going to use you."

He bent his head and took her mouth, his kiss hard and demanding and she hated him, hated the touch of his hands, the feel of his mouth.

Hated, hated, hated…and then she stopped thinking and fell into the kiss.

He felt it happen. Knew the moment she let go—and then his arms were around her, she was in his lap, his hand was under her sweater, his mouth was feeding on hers and it was as it had been that night, the hot need, the drowning passion, the desire to take and take and never let her go…

His cell phone rang.

Slowly, Alex came back to the world. The car had stopped. He cupped Maria's shoulders, put her from him. Her eyes opened slowly; he saw in them everything he'd seen that night. Surprise. Desire. Even the innocence he damned well knew wasn't real.

Angrily, he yanked the phone from his pocket and flipped it open.

"Alexandros? Are you there?"

His father's voice buzzed in his ear. *"Ne,"* he said, clearing his throat. Aegeus talked. Alex listened. Yes, he said again, yes, all right.

But his eyes never left Maria's face. The way she was looking at him, the way her lips were parted. He wanted to reach for her when the call ended. She knew it; he could see it, feel it. She was ready for him. God, yes, she was ready.

But he wasn't a fool. *He* would be in control this time, not she.

The Mercedes slowed. Ahead, elaborate wrought-iron security gates swung slowly open. The car moved under a long archway of tall cedars and came to a stop in a circular drive before a magnificent glass and cedar mansion.

"Where are we?" Maria said warily.

"Bluebeard's castle," Alex said wryly. "My home, Maria. My housekeeper expects you. Go inside. See if everything is as you wish."

"I don't under—"

"There's been a change of plans. I have work to do. I'll be back this evening. Six o'clock. We have a dinner appointment. Be ready. I do not like to be kept waiting."

The commands were flung at her like stones from a slingshot. Maria lifted her chin and glared.

"I have no interest in playing games, Your Highness, or going on pretend dates."

A smile spread across his lips. "In such a hurry to get to bed, *glyka mou*?" Her cheeks colored and he gave the kind of laugh she knew she would never forget. "It's hardly a date," he said brusquely. "My parents want to meet the winner of the royal commission." He wrapped his hand around the back of her neck, drew her to him and kissed her, hard and deep. "One final reprieve, *agapimeni*, and then, rest assured, you will share my bed."

CHAPTER SEVEN

ALEX'S driver deposited Maria's suitcase beside her, saluted briskly and strode back to the limousine.

Wait, Maria almost said, but what would be the point? There was something intimidating about being delivered to the massive front doors of a mansion where she knew no one, but getting back into the car beside a man who'd just kissed her senseless wasn't much of an alternative.

She could hear the purr of the big car's engine as it went down the drive. She took a deep breath, raised a hand toward the bell. The doors swung open before she could touch it and a small woman dressed head to toe in crisp black cotton stood looking at her.

Wonderful. This had to be the housekeeper. Did she bear more than a passing resemblance to the one in that old movie about Young Frankenstein? Then the woman smiled, dipped a knee, and was instantly transformed from wicked witch to a welcoming committee of one.

"*Kalimera, Keeria. Onomázome Athenia.*"

"I'm afraid I don't speak Greek—"

"Of course. Forgive me. Good morning, madam, and welcome. I am Athenia. The prince has told me to make sure you are comfortable."

Did he leave the same orders for all his mistresses?

"Thank you."

Athenia clapped her hands. A manservant appeared, inclined his head to Maria and scooped up her suitcase.

"Really," Maria said, with a little laugh, "no one has to bow to me. I'm not a royal or anything like that."

"You are the prince's guest and the lady who is to create a beautiful gift for our beloved queen. We are honored by your presence, *keeria*." The housekeeper stepped back. "Please, won't you come in?"

What would happen to Athenia's warm welcome if she knew that Alex's esteemed guest had also made a devil's bargain with him? There was no sense in thinking about it. She was here, and she would do what had to be done.

"Thank you," Maria said again, and stepped

into a cool, slate-floored entryway. One quick glance assured her this house would never be confused with Bluebeard's castle.

"Would you like something to drink? Something to eat? I know you have had a long journey."

Just the mention of food and Maria's belly did a nasty little flip-flop.

"No," she said quickly, "no, thank you. I'm not hungry."

"Then, would you like me to show you to your room?" Athenia nodded toward a spiraling staircase that seemed suspended in the air. "Or would you prefer to see your workshop first?"

Her room? What the housekeeper meant was the prince's room. Unbidden, a tremor of what surely had to be apprehension danced along Maria's skin.

"Uh, no," she said, a little breathlessly. "I mean…I mean, my workshop will be here?"

"It will. I hope you will like it. His Highness gave very specific orders but we had so little time…"

The Prince of Arrogance's specialty, Maria thought grimly. Handing out orders. Giving people little time to obey, much less question. And why would she be working here? What had he done? Put a bench in the basement? Hung a work light over it?

She'd have everything she needed, he'd said.

"If you would please come this way...?"

Maria followed the housekeeper through a series of magnificent, high-ceilinged rooms. Despite her irritation, the artist in her could not help but see the house's incredible beauty.

The lifestyles of the rich and famous, she thought wryly. Always and forever amazing.

She knew how they lived. She was a New Yorker; her life and those of the fantastically wealthy were completely separate but, in Manhattan, you brushed shoulders all the time even if it was only at the Bobbi Brown counter at Saks. And if you knew somebody who knew somebody who knew somebody who could get you into a promotional party for *Vogue* or *Vanity Fair*—and she did—you could even get up-close-and-personal glimpses of that kind of storied existence. An old classmate from FIT, a guy who now designed incredible floral displays, had edged her onto a couple of those guest lists, though attending the parties had never snagged her a client.

Still, nothing she'd seen compared to this.

Maria tried not to stare as she followed

Athenia through Alex's home. The mansion was spectacular but she had to give him grudging credit. It had not been built to impress, though it surely did, but to celebrate the wooded setting, the sapphire bay, the white sand beach. Walls were made of glass. Almost all the rooms had terraces or balconies, and the water from an enormous infinity pool seemed to spill into a sea that stretched to the horizon.

Athenia led her out a pair of glass French doors. Apparently, her workshop was not in the house. Maybe the mighty prince thought she could make his mother's birthday gift in the garage, Maria thought irritably as they made their way along a flagstone path that wound through a dormant garden.

The housekeeper turned to her and smiled.

"Your workshop, *keeria*."

Maria blinked in surprise.

Ahead, in a grove of firs, stood a perfect miniature of the main house. Wood. Glass. Soaring rooflines, terraces, white sand and blue water a dizzying distance below.

"This is normally a guesthouse but the prince was very specific about your needs. We worked quickly to meet them, but if anything is not to your liking…"

Not to her liking? Maria almost laughed as they stepped inside.

The guesthouse had three rooms. A bedroom. A marble bathroom. And a main room, big and high-ceilinged and brightly lit, a room that had been filled with oak worktables and benches, with shelves that held tools she had dreamed of buying but only in a distant, far more affluent future. A quick glance revealed heated presses, torches, hand tools and protective gear, all of it straight out of a jewelry maker's dreams.

And there were cabinets.

Cabinets with drawers and cubby-holes and shelves. Cabinets that opened to reveal all the things she could possibly need to create Queen Tia's necklace. Waxes. Molds. Polishes. Trays of bright gold and platinum and silver.

And one special tray that made her heartbeat quicken.

"Shall I leave you here, miss?" Athenia said.

Maria nodded. And reached for that special tray. Lined in black silk, its small compartments burned with the fire of the brilliant white and pink diamonds she had so carefully described in her proposal as the only ones suitable for the queen's gift.

The stones glittered with life.

Carefully matched white diamonds from a mine in the Canadian Yukon, where there was no danger of them having been involved in the blood conflicts of the world. And two magnificent pink diamonds, so exquisite they could only be from the fabulous mines of Calista.

Maria lifted the pink stones from their silken compartments. She would only use one as the centerpiece of the necklace. In her proposal, she'd pointed out that pink diamonds, that all diamonds, had slight differences in color.

Obviously, King Aegeus had decided to provide her with two stones so she could choose the one she preferred. The implications of such wealth were almost beyond comprehension.

The pinks were easily forty karats each, just as she had requested. She had determined the size she'd need by estimating that the Stefani diamond, in its original form, was said to have weighed approximately one hundred and ninety carats, meaning it had been even bigger than the fabled Darya-ye Noor, a pale pink diamond that had been mined in India hundreds of years ago and then became part of the Persian crown jewels.

Thus, the half of the Stefani pink diamond now in the Aristan crown would weigh somewhere around eighty carats, since some material would have been lost when the stone was split. The pink diamond that would be the focal point in the queen's necklace would have to be of a size to complement the one in the crown.

These incredible pink ovals would look the same to the untrained eye, but Maria could see a slight variation in color. The only way to choose the proper stone for the queen's necklace would be to check both against the pink diamond in the crown. The palace had provided her with photos of it but no photo could capture the soul of a diamond, or the subtleties of its color, especially when it was half of the legendary Stefani stone.

Carefully, she returned the pink diamonds to their tray. Her design couldn't be changed now, nor did she want to change it, but diamonds, born in the extreme pressure and heat of the earth's forming crust millions of years ago, all had their own characteristics. Her plans needed simple refining. Nothing anyone but she would notice. A filigree of gold here, a millimeter less in depth there.

First, though, she had to call Joaquin and Sela and let them know she was all right. She hadn't had the chance to do it last night...

Better not to think about that.

She used her cell phone, left a brief message about the commission on their voice mail, with no mention of the very personal contract terms that involved the prince.

"I'm very happy," she said. And, at the moment, that was the truth. She had the perfect workshop. The best tools. And the most magnificent diamonds imaginable.

Maria hitched her hip onto a stool, pulled a pad and pencil toward her and began to sketch. Yes, she thought as she lost herself in the work she loved, she could make her design even more pleasing to the eye. And thinking about diamonds was far safer than thinking about the man to whom she'd all but sold herself. The man who would claim her later tonight, who would take her to his bed, make love to her as he had all those weeks ago. She would hold back, hold back…but, in the end, she knew she would sob his name, open her mouth, her body to his. She would be lost in his arms, in his strength and beauty and passion.

She forced the treacherous thoughts from her mind, put all her energy into her ideas for the necklace and the diamonds. They, at least, would never hurt her.

The sun shifted in the sky. She never noticed.

She sketched, erased, sketched… And yawned. Yawned again. She was tired all the time lately. This time, at least there was a reason. It had to be jet lag, catching up to her.

As she had done many times over the last couple of weeks, Maria set her work aside, folded her arms on the table, lowered her head and rested her cheek on them.

Just a few seconds, to clear the cobwebs from her brain, she thought. Just a few seconds…

Jet lag, Alex kept telling himself. That was why he felt so damned irritable.

Besides, it was unreasonable for his father to have demanded a meeting now, but that was Aegeus's way. What the king wished, others must do. And today, this very afternoon, what Aegeus wished was to meet with his three sons and discuss plans for the construction of another high-rise complex in Ellos.

There was no point to such a discussion.

For one thing, the construction was already underway. For another, Alex was in charge of the project. He had taken over development on Aristo more than eight years ago, with Aegeus's grudging blessing.

"You might as well get some use out of that

MBA of yours," he'd said, which was as close as he'd ever come to acknowledging that his second son was now more qualified than he to oversee the kingdom's booming economy.

This meeting was just a not so subtle reminder that Aegeus was still Aegeus, Alex thought as he sat at the conference table in the king's palace office. As if any of them could ever forget that.

"…twenty stories, Alexandros, but why not thirty?"

Alex looked up from the doodles he'd been making on the yellow notepad before him. Aegeus's eyes were focused on him. His younger brother, Andreas, seated beside him, nudged Alex's foot with his under the table. His older brother, Sebastian, seated opposite, raised his eyebrows.

"Didn't you say the architect agrees that twenty stories for the center building would be right, Alex?" he said smoothly.

"Yes," Andreas chimed in, "twenty stories so that the view of the harbor would not be blocked from the condominium complex on the heights, right, Alex?"

"That's correct," Alex replied. Sebastian grinned. *You owe us, big time,* that grin said. Well, hell. That was how it had always been, the three brothers bailing each other out of hot water when their father turned a stern eye on any one of them.

Aegeus looked grim, but then he looked that way most of the time. He looked tired, too, Alex noticed, and thinner than usual.

"Are you feeling all right, Father?" he said.

The king's eyes narrowed. "I'm feeling fine, thank you," he said brusquely. "Fine enough to ask a few more questions—that is, if you can manage to keep your attention on our discussion a bit longer."

Alex felt a muscle knot in his jaw. "What else do you want to know, Father?"

"Have you settled the woman in?"

"Excuse me?"

"The woman, Mary Santos. Is she settled in?"

"Her name is Maria," Alex said carefully. "And I thought we were talking about the Ellos convention center."

"We were. Now we're talking about the person who'll make your mother's gift. What is she like?"

"She is, ah, she is talented."

Talented, indeed.

"I assumed that," his father said impatiently. "But what is she *like*? I am to meet her tonight, at dinner. Will she be able to carry on a conversation with some intelligence, or is she one of those leftover flower children who walks around barefoot?"

Sebastian coughed. Andreas cleared his throat. Alex shot them both looks that promised trouble when they were alone.

"She's a designer, Father," he said carefully. "A New Yorker. I'm sure you'll find her interesting and able to hold her own at the dinner table."

And more than able to hold her own everywhere else. In bed, for instance, where he should have been with her, right now.

"I assume you've put her in a suite at The Grand Hotel."

"No." Alex hesitated. "I, ah, I decided to keep her at my house at Apollonia."

His father stared at him. So did his brothers. *Damn it,* Alex thought, and felt heat rise in his face.

"Security," he said quickly. "She'll be working with a fortune in diamonds."

"Have we security problems at The Grand?"

"No, of course not. But there are so many tourists…"

"Tourists who pay a thousand Euros a night for a room are not tourists likely to dabble in theft," Aegeus said, his words heavy with sarcasm.

There was a moment's silence. Then Sebastian and Andreas spoke at the same time.

"You can never be too sure," Andreas said.

"Remember that incident in—where was it, Alex? Some hotel in Manhattan?"

His brothers had redeemed themselves. "Exactly," Alex said. "Security is much better at my place. The gates. The electronics. The guards. I had my guesthouse converted into a workshop for her."

Aegeus nodded. "Well. Well, yes. Good thinking."

A compliment. Something rare. Of course, it was a compliment given in response to a lie. He'd placed Maria in his home for reasons that didn't have a thing to do with anything but lust.

He liked women. He liked sex. He knew what desire was, how anticipation could enhance the moment when a man finally took a woman.

But he'd never behaved like this.

Demanding Maria's compliance. Damned near forcing her to agree to sleep with him. It had made sense, when he'd planned it. He would use her for his own ends as she had used him—

If that was true, why was his body in this almost constant state of arousal? He'd spent the last hours thinking about her. Imagining her waiting for his arrival. Imagining what he would do when he reached home.

The images, hot and raw, flooded his mind. If he didn't do something soon, he was going to explode.

"Alex? Are you listening to me? I said—"

"Father." Alex pushed back his chair and got to his feet. "I'm sorry, but I have to leave."

Aegeus looked at him in disbelief. "You what?"

"I said I have to—"

"We have not finished discussing the convention center."

"We finished discussing it three months ago," Alex said crisply.

His father glared at him. "I don't like your tone."

"My apologies, Father. I'm exhausted, that's all. I've flown to New York and back in, what, less than twenty-four hours." He forced a smile. "Perhaps we can put off this conversation until tomorrow."

Aegeus studied his middle son, then nodded.

"Very well." He rose from his chair. Sebastian and Andreas immediately did the same. "Be prompt for dinner tonight, please. All of you. Alex, tell Ms. Santos your mother and I look forward to meeting her."

Alex started toward the door. The king called after him.

"Alex? My initial concern about this woman, on reading her proposal, was that she was too young and inexperienced. Now that you've spent a bit of time with her, what do you think? How does she strike you?"

Spectacularly beautiful. And spectacularly immoral. And, *Thee mou*, so desirable he ached to possess her.

"I told you," Alex said calmly. "She's very interesting."

Then he got the hell out of there before his father or, worse, his brothers could ask him any more questions.

The drive home seemed to last an eternity, even though he was at the wheel of his Ferrari and took both the highway and then the winding road to the house at breakneck speed.

Would she be waiting for him? He'd told her to be ready by six; he was an hour early. She might be in the bath. Or undressing, baring her flesh to the waning afternoon light.

Such schoolboy fantasies, and completely demolished when Athenia told him Keeria Santos was in the guesthouse. In the workshop.

The workshop, he thought as he strode down

the path to it. Of course. The only allegiance, the only honesty she had was to her work.

It filled him with a rage he knew had no basis in reality.

She should have been in the house. In his bedroom. Dressing for dinner, as he'd told her to. Or waiting for him. For his touch. For the act that would avenge what she had done to him weeks ago.

"Maria," he barked as he flung open the guest-house door. "Maria, I told you…"

And he saw her. At the workbench. Her head on her arms. Asleep.

His anger drained away. He felt something new take its place, something he could not name and he swallowed hard, closed the door quietly and stood watching her. Then, slowly, he walked to her.

Her head was turned to the side. Her lashes formed dark crescents against the high arc of her cheekbones; there were purple smudges of exhaustion under her eyes.

My fault, he thought. He had walked into her life…hell, he had bullied his way into her life, then dragged her halfway around the world. Not that he owed her more delicate treatment. It was just that she looked so innocent in her sleep. Her lustrous hair, lying tumbled over one shoulder. Her translucent skin. Her lips, delicately curved.

He could remember their taste.

Not from that last kiss he'd given her hours ago, a kiss given in rage. He remembered her taste from that night in Ellos. How her mouth had trembled beneath his. How her sigh of surrender had mingled with his breath. How he had groaned at the sweetness of her.

He didn't think. Didn't question. Instead, he bent down, brushed a soft, silken curl from her cheek. Put his lips to her temple. The pink shell of her ear. The curve of her jaw.

"Maria." Her name was a whisper. "Maria," he said again, and when she sighed, he squatted beside her and pressed his lips gently to hers.

Her lashes fluttered.

He kissed her again. Her taste was honeyed. *Don't,* he thought, *don't.* But what could be wrong with one more kiss? One more sip of nectar from her soft, rosy mouth? Just one last brush of his lips against hers. Just one... And this time, her lips parted to his. Clung lightly to his. Her eyes opened; her pupils were huge and dark.

"Alexandros?" she whispered, and he was lost.

Groaning, he scooped her into his arms.

Brought her down on the soft Kilim carpet. Swept his hands into her hair, lifted her lovely face to his, and took possession of her mouth.

"Alexandros," she sighed.

His name. Not any other man's. His. Only his, and now her arms were around his neck, her mouth was moving on his as he lay her back and came down beside her.

His hands cupped her face. Her beauty stole his breath; the smile that trembled on her lips pierced his heart.

"Yes," he said huskily. "That's right, *glyka mou.* Say my name."

She did, again and again until he silenced her with a deep, hungry kiss. A cry rose in her throat. Her arms tightened around him. Her back arched; she rose against him and he groaned again and slipped his hand inside her black tights.

Her flesh was warm. Soft. Fragrant with the glorious scent of arousal.

He could feel the race of his blood.

He put his lips to her throat.

She sobbed his name. Cupped the back of his head. Urged his mouth down, down, to the uptilted thrust of her breast. To the pebbled nipple that pressed against the softness of her sweater. He caught the bud lightly between his teeth. Her cry pierced the thick silence.

"Yes," she said, "yes, yes..."

He pushed up the sweater. Sucked a nipple into his mouth. She was lifting herself to him, burying her fingers in his hair, urging him closer, closer...

A knock, as strident as Olympian thunder, sounded at the door. Alex barely heard it but Maria stiffened in his arms.

"Alex," she hissed.

"Shh, *agapi mou*. Never mind. Whoever is there will go away."

The knock came again. "Your Highness?" Athenia's voice was thin and apologetic. "Your mother is on the phone. She asks if you and Keeria Santos would come by a few minutes early."

Alex pressed his forehead to Maria's. "Yes," he called, "all right. Tell the queen we'll be there as soon as we can." He waited until he was sure the housekeeper was gone. Until he could move without disgracing himself. Then he sat up. "We'll finish this later," he started to say, but Maria had already rolled away from him and risen to her feet. Her face was white except for two spots of crimson high on her cheeks.

"Is that how you get your women, Your

Highness? By taking advantage of them when they're asleep?"

Her voice shook with indignation. Hell, he was shaking, too, but with thwarted desire.

"You know that isn't how it was."

"What I know," she said, the words laced with accusation, "is that I woke up and found you all over me!"

He stood and faced her, caught between equal parts of anger and frustration.

"Liar," he said in a low voice.

She turned her back. He grasped her shoulder and swung her toward him.

"What's the matter, *glyka mou*? Don't you like it when the tables are turned? When you're not in control of the situation?"

"All right," she snapped. "You made your point. You—you got me to—to give in to you. Are you satisfied now?"

He gave a sharp, ugly laugh. "We have a long way to go until I'm satisfied, sweetheart."

The crimson drained from her face. "How can you do this?"

It was, he thought, an excellent question.

Despite everything, he was not a man who would ever take an unwilling woman to bed. That was part of the problem, when he came down to it. Maria said she didn't want him but each time he took her in his arms, she turned that into a lie. Or did she?

Was she still playing him? Was she using him now, even as he was determined to use her? And how could he tell himself that was what he was doing when the truth was he had never wanted a woman as he wanted her and—*be honest, Karedes*—and revenge or payback, whatever name he gave his supposed motivation, had zero to do with what he felt once she was in his arms.

He turned away from her. Ran his hand through his thick, dark hair.

He was a man who had always prided himself on logic. On self-discipline. And right now, hell, who was he kidding? Ever since the night he'd first met this woman, logic and self-discipline had gone by the wayside.

Maybe it was enough to admit that he wanted her still, and that at the end of a month she would be out of his system. Damned right, she would, he thought grimly, and he turned and faced her again.

"I suggest you return to the house," he said brusquely. "One of the maids has unpacked your suitcase. You have—" He glanced at his watch. "You have twenty minutes to get ready and then we leave for the palace."

Her chin came up. "Where has your devoted slave put my things?"

Thee mou, she enraged him! He wanted to shake her. Or strip her naked and show her who was in charge here.

"Your clothes are where they belong," he snapped. "In my room. We have an agreement, Ms. Santos, that says you are to fulfill your required duties in their entirety, or have you conveniently forgotten that?"

She gave him a withering look. "How could I forget what is sure to be the worst agreement of my life?"

It was, Maria thought, a fine line.

But the Prince of Arrogance only laughed, and that was the sound that followed her all the way to the house.

CHAPTER EIGHT

WHAT did you wear to dine with royalty?

Probably nothing she'd packed, Maria thought unhappily as she followed Athenia to Alex's bedroom.

Bedroom? Could you call a room this size a bedroom? It was bigger than her loft. Polished wood floors. Handmade rugs. A cathedral ceiling. Skylights. A wall of glass and, beyond it, a terrace and the pool that seemed to hang suspended over the bay.

And a bed.

A bed centered beneath the skylights, elevated on a raised platform, covered by a black silk comforter and a sea of black and white pillows as if it were a stage set.

"Madam will find her things hung in the dressing room."

Maria swung toward Athenia. "Yes. I—I— Thank you."

"Everything has been pressed, *keeria*, to your liking, I hope."

"Thank you," she said again. They seemed the only words she could manage.

The housekeeper smiled politely and shut the door behind her. Maria waited a couple of seconds, then turned the lock. She leaned back against the door, shut her eyes and inhaled deeply.

It was a handsome room. Hell, it was a magnificent room. And that bed...

Do not look at that bed, Maria. Do not even think about it.

She would not. She would shower and dress. She had twenty minutes. Not much time, but enough. Actually, she never took longer than that to get ready for a date. Except, this wasn't a date. It was business. Business to be conducted at a palace.

She'd seen the palace—from the outside, anyway—the last time she was here.

It made Buckingham Palace look small.

"That's it," she whispered. "Work yourself into a panic. That's going to be a huge help!" Spine straight, she ignored the bed and marched across the room. This was an important night.

Indeed, it was. At the end of it, Alex was going to make love to her.

Maria rolled her eyes. It was stupid to let her thoughts wander. Of course, tonight was important. She had the commission; now, she had to make sure she had the hearts and minds of her clients.

Her clients. The king of Aristo and his queen. She'd come a long way from the phony Frenchman of *L'Orangerie*.

The dressing room made her laugh. Add some plumbing and most Manhattan residents would have happily called it an apartment. And there were her things, on a rack all by themselves, surrounded by other racks filled with men's clothes. Alex's clothes.

And no, she was not going to think about that now. Dinner was everything. It had to go well.

Her clothes, as Athenia had told her, had been pressed, hung and organized by color. Giddy laughter rose in her throat. Jeans and jeans and jeans, T-shirts and blouses and sweaters. Organized and pressed, and what in hell was there hanging in front of her she could wear to a palace?

Casual, Alex had said. Easy for him to say. And to do.

What was he going to wear? And where would he shower and dress?

Not here, and that was all that mattered. For all she knew, he kept a complete wardrobe in each bedroom. A mistress in each, too. Or maybe this was the way installing a new mistress was handled. Maybe his staff was trained to move some of the master's clothes, just enough to get his latest conquest through the confusion of her first night here.

Stop it, Maria thought furiously.

She was most assuredly not Alex's conquest, she was his— What would be the correct word? Never mind. She would not dwell on how or why she was in his bedroom, or the implications of it, either—or on the fact that his entire staff surely now understood she would be sleeping with him.

A dozen other women probably had gone this route. She lacked their experience in the art or business of being a kept woman but instinct told her that a woman who filled that role would not blush at such information being public.

She'd do her best not to blush, either.

Besides, Alex would not 'keep' her. The money for the commission didn't come from him. It was for the design and execution of the queen's birthday gift, and she would not accept so much as a penny for anything else.

A phone rang.

Maria looked around. There it was. A small white telephone on the wall of the dressing room. It rang again and she plucked it from its cradle, put it to her ear and said a careful, "Hello?"

"You're down to twelve minutes, *glyka mou*."

"Alexandros?"

"I like it when you call me that."

His voice was husky. Why did that roughness always send a tingle along her skin?

"Alexandros!" She looked around wildly. "Where are you?"

He laughed. "Relax, sweetheart. I can't see you—but I know exactly what you're doing. You're standing in the middle of my bedroom, trying not to look at the bed and wondering what on earth possessed you to bring nothing suitable to wear this evening."

She blinked. "Wrong," she said airily. After all, she was in the dressing room, not the bedroom, and she'd already wasted time trying not to look at the bed.

"Try the emerald silk dress and the black stiletto sandals. And before you tell me you won't wear another woman's cast-offs, let me assure you they aren't. The dress and shoes were both delivered from the Chanel boutique in Ellos a couple of hours before we arrived." His words took on that same sexy softness again. "I had to guess at the size, *glyka mou*, so I hope I got them right. Of course, we won't have any such difficulties after tonight."

Maria felt her entire body blush as she slammed the phone back onto its cradle. How dared he buy her clothes? Did he really think she'd wear anything he'd paid for?

There it was. The dress. And right below it, the shoes. Both were gorgeous. The brilliant color of the dress would be perfect with the delicately spiked heels. Exactly what she'd have bought for an occasion like this…if she'd been in a position to spend, what, ten thousand bucks?

She would not wear these things.

She would wear something of her own.

Black jeans. A white silk blouse. Dressy enough for dinner at an upscale New York restaurant…but for dinner at a palace? For what was, basically, a business meeting that was surely going to change her life?

"Damn you, Alexandros," she said bitterly—and knew she had lost Round One.

She showered quickly, and never mind that the faint, clean scent of the hand-milled soap reminded her of Alex. The shampoo had the same effect. So what? Soap was soap, shampoo was shampoo. She towel-dried her hair—no time for anything else—and hurried into the dressing room.

There were more than shoes with the dress. There was a tiny black evening purse. And undies. A black lace bra. A black lace thong. The sheerest thigh-high nylons she'd ever seen.

She had her own underwear.

But not like this.

To hell with it.

She put on the bits of black lace, the sheer stockings. Hair loose or up? Maria peered into the mirror. Up. The mass of dark strands was too damp, too wild, too curly to leave loose. Finally, she slipped on the emerald silk dress. Stepped into the black sandals.

And saw herself in the mirror.

He had good taste, the Prince of Arrogance, she thought wryly. A career as a personal shopper could be his in the blink of an eye.

The dress was a perfect fit, demure and businesslike even as it made the most of her slender figure. The shoes were gorgeous. Straps that wound around her foot. Stiletto heels as thin as the blade for which they were named.

Could he possibly know shoes were her weakness?

No, she thought. The better probability was that they were *his* weakness. Maybe later tonight, he'd want her in the stilettos and nothing besides the black lace thong…

"Oh God," she whispered, and felt her heart rate shoot into the stratosphere.

Jewelry, she thought numbly, because it was safer to think about that than about what happened to her body each time she imagined being in this room, in that bed, with the gorgeous Alexandros. How could you hate a man and still want him?

A question for another time, not for the one minute—the *one* minute she had left!

Fortunately, she'd dumped a couple of pieces of her stuff into her handbag. A twisted gold chain? No. A shorter one, intricately braided? No. A slender gold rope with a hunk of polished amber knotted at the center? Yes. Perfect. Small gold hoops in her ears. Had she forgotten anything? She certainly had. A quick swipe of mascara. Sheer cherry lip gloss. A dab of powder on her suddenly shiny nose.

She took a steadying breath. Another. *Ready or not,* she thought, and she unlocked the bedroom door.

He was right outside it, waiting for her.

'Gorgeous' was the wrong word to describe him. 'Spectacular' came closer, but it still didn't quite cover it.

Say something, Maria told herself, but her brain was numb. She could only look at him as he stood leaning back against the cypress balustrade that enclosed the open loft, arms folded, ankles crossed, the very portrait of The Male Waiting for his Date. He wore a grey jacket, a black open-necked shirt, black trousers and darkest brown mocs. His hair was damp; he was freshly shaven...

He was beautiful. The in-the-flesh subject of a woman's dreams, except she didn't have dreams like those. Well, not until after that night they'd made love. Correction. That night they'd had sex, and look where that had led.

He said nothing. Showed nothing. Slowly, slowly enough to make her wonder if the dress didn't look as good as she thought, his gaze traveled from the top of her head all the way to her toes, then back up again.

That was when he smiled. A slow, lazy, purely masculine curve of his lips that sent shock waves through her blood.

"Just one thing..." He reached out, took the

clip from her hair and let all the wild curls tumble to her shoulders. "Perfect," he said softly.

She had to stop herself from returning the compliment. Instead, she tossed her head as if it meant nothing. Damned if that didn't make him grin.

"Shall we?" he said, holding out his hand.

Maria ignored the offer, brushed past him and went down the stairs.

His car was a low-slung, snarling crimson beast.

A Maserati. A Lamborghini. A Ferrari. One of those, she was certain, but what would a born-and-bred New Yorker know? Subway trains, yes. Automobiles, no. The only certainty was that he drove fast, too fast, with a macho assurance that she tried not to let impress her.

But it did.

Was there a female alive who wouldn't be impressed by a man so beautiful it hurt to look at him, driving a car that rumbled like a big, predatory animal? One hand was curved over the steering wheel. The other rested lightly on the gear shift lever.

Such competent hands. So powerful. His hands had been all over her the night they'd met. She could still feel them, if she closed her eyes. His fingertips playing with her nipples. His thumbs gently parting her labia. Her shocked cries that had quickly turned to sobs of ecstasy.

She felt the instant bloom of warmth between her thighs.

"Something the matter?"

His voice startled her. She looked at him and thought it was a good thing he didn't have X-ray vision or he'd see straight through her clothes, see that she was wet, that her nipples were peaked.

"Maria?"

I want you, she thought dizzily, *that's what's the matter.*

"Are you worried about dinner tonight?"

No, she thought, on a faint wave of hysteria, *not dinner.*

"Don't be. This is just my family."

Dinner. She had to remember that. He was talking about dinner.

"Oh," she said, and caught her bottom lip between her teeth.

Alex felt his muscles contract. Did she have to look so beautiful? Did she have to worry her lip that way? Damn it, this was not good. He should never have kissed her in the guesthouse. He'd taken two cold showers before he got dressed and he was still hard with wanting her.

What if he pulled the car over, took her in his

arms and nipped that sweet bottom lip himself? Just lightly enough to make her moan and sigh and beg him…

"Family?" she said, and he blinked.

"Uh, yes. Family. My older brother, Sebastian. My baby brother, Andreas. My sister Katarina— everyone calls her Kitty. The only one missing will be Elissa. She's in Paris."

"So many people?"

The tip of her tongue slicked over that softly bitten, now undoubtedly sensitive bottom lip. By the time they reached the palace, he'd be completely out of his mind. When had this woman assumed such power over him? It made him angry, and his words were more harsh than he'd intended.

"Don't tell me you're nervous about meeting royalty, *glyka mou*. After all, you did fine with me the first time out."

She swung toward him.

"I told you, I didn't know who you were."

"Right. You just happened to meet me on the street and when I suggested we go to bed, you said, hey, I have nothing else to do, so why not?"

It hadn't been like that and he knew it. She'd been sweetly innocent; he'd seduced her with words, with caresses, with a need unlike any he'd ever experienced in all his thirty-one years. Except, it had all been a lie. She'd set him up. *She* had seduced him…

Hadn't she?

"You know what, Alex?" she said, her voice shaking. "You're a real bastard!"

She was right. What was between them was personal and had nothing to do with this evening's gathering. Tonight was about plans for the national celebration of his mother's birthday. Affairs of state came before everything else, a truth that had always been part of his life.

"Okay. Let's start over. Ask me again about who'll be at dinner tonight."

Maria stared straight ahead. Alex sighed in resignation.

"You need to know these things, *glyka mou*. How else to prepare for the sight of Sebastian, who stands four feet tall and weighs three hundred pounds? Or to know that Andreas is in *The Guinness Book of World Records* for Worst Footballer of the Year?"

She swung toward him, as he'd hoped she would. "What?"

Alex grinned. "Don't panic. We still tease Andreas over the time he missed six consecutive tries in a game—but we leave out the fact that he was only five years old at the time. As for Sebastian…" His grin broadened. "The truth is, except for a lack of hair anyplace but his knuckles and back, he's not bad-looking. Well, he's not as handsome as I am, of course…"

He couldn't be.

Alex was joking, Maria knew. Still, what he'd said about being handsome was true. He was, without question, the most beautiful man she'd ever seen… And what did that have to do with anything? He was still exactly what she'd called him. No-good, self-centered and arrogant, and if she had not called him all those names yet, she surely would before the evening ended.

She sat back, folded her hands in her lap and told herself she'd get through whatever lay ahead because she had no other choice.

The Ferrari paused before the high gates outside the palace. A smartly uniformed soldier stepped from the guardhouse, approached, looked in at Alex, shot straight as a ramrod and delivered a perfect salute.

"Your Highness."

"Stavros. It's good to see you pretending to be a soldier again." Maria looked at Alex in surprise. The soldier, still saluting, went on staring directly ahead. "Especially since we both know I can out-run, out-shoot, out-anything you choose when we have the chance to give it another try."

The soldier's lips twitched. "Your Highness is, as usual, full of, ah, full of air. Sir."

Alex laughed and returned the salute. "At ease, Stavros. Good to see you back. The ankle's okay?"

The soldier grinned. "It's fine, sir. And your shoulder?"

"Good to go. You signed up for the next Games?"

"Absolutely, sir. And you?"

"Try and keep me away," Alex said, smiling.

Another smart salute; the gates opened and they drove slowly down a wide, tree-lined avenue toward the broad marble steps that led to the front doors of the palace.

"You and that man know each other?" Maria said.

"For years. We went to nursery school together." He smiled. "My mother's modernist ideas won out that time. My father thought it was a mistake to educate me among what he tried not to call the commoners."

"But he didn't—I mean, the way he addressed you—"

"What's the problem, sweetheart? Disappointed to find out some people don't think of me as you do?"

He pulled up before the steps. A valet opened his door; another did the same for Maria. Ahead, the enormous entry doors swung open. To Maria's surprise, she saw the world-famous King Aegeus and Queen Tia in the doorway.

"They asked me to bring you in through the Grand Hall," Alex said softly as he moved around the car to stand beside her. "And they're greeting you themselves. We are not as formal as some royal houses but still, this is an honor." He offered her his arm. "Take it," he said softly, "and smile, or my parents will think you hate me. And you don't hate me, *glyka mou*. We both know that."

"Wrong," Maria said sweetly. "But why should I take it out on them?"

She put her hand lightly on his arm, took a deep breath, and let him lead her up the steps.

"…and so," Princess Kitty said, "Alex convinced me that it was my royal obligation to sneak into the butler's pantry to find out what our parents had bought us for Christmas—well, it wasn't a butler's pantry anymore, of course, it was just this huge room we store stuff in at the beach house at Kionia—has Alex told you about Kionia? Oh, it's this incredible stretch of land overlooking the Strait of Poseidon that separates us from Calista, and our house is big and old and beautiful, and it's all very laid-back, you know, I can go around dressed casually—"

"Sloppily, you mean," Aegeus said, his tone harsh. "And why are we boring our guest with talk of childish pranks done years ago?"

The family dining room became silent. Kitty's round, pretty face turned crimson. "Of course. Ms. Santos, my apologies."

"Oh, please, don't apologize." Without thinking, Maria reached for the princess's hand. "It's lovely to hear stories like that. My own childhood wasn't as much fun. No brothers. No sisters." Suddenly, she realized that every eye was on her, and that she was hanging onto Kitty's hand as if it belonged to Sela and not a princess. Flushed, she let go. "I mean—I mean, this has been such a lovely evening…You've all been so—so—"

"It's been our pleasure, Ms. Santos," the queen said gently.

"Please, won't you all call me Maria?"

"Maria." Tia smiled. "I hope you intend to see some of our island in the next few weeks."

Maria shot a glance at Alex, who was calmly drinking his coffee. "If I have the chance."

"I'm fascinated by the thought of such a slip of a girl designing and making such a magnificent necklace. I understand Alex has outfitted a workshop for you in his home on the coast."

"Yes." This time, Maria didn't dare look at Alex. "He has."

"And is it to your liking?"

What was the sense in lying? "Very much so, Your Majesty. In fact, it's better equipped than my own place in New York."

"Good. If you should need anything more—"

"Well, I do need something. A couple of things, actually…"

"Such as?"

"Some information, to start. I understand that King Christos ordered the Stefani diamond, which had been the centerpiece of the crown of Adamas, to be split in two."

She could almost feel the sudden tension in the room.

"I fail to see why the history of Adamas should be under discussion," the king said stiffly.

Maria cleared her throat. "I don't mean to pry, Your Majesty. It's only that knowing the history of the diamond will help me in creating the necklace."

"Nonsense. Gold and diamonds well help, not timeworn stories about the Stefani diamond and the islands of Aristo and Calista."

Silence. Then Maria felt Alex clasp her hand under cover of the table and enfold it in his own.

"Maria is an artist, Father. Her creations are, in a sense, representations of a life force—in this case, a celebration of Mother's birthday as well as the continuity of our people. She's simply trying to gain some understanding of our kingdom. Isn't that right, Maria?"

"Yes," she said, staring at Alex, amazed he should instinctively comprehend what most people did not. "Stories, legends, history…those are some of the qualities my work is meant to convey."

"Well, our history isn't very complicated," Sebastian said pleasantly. "The Kingdom of Adamas dates back to ancient Rome and Greece."

"Yes," Maria said again. "Alex told me it did."

"Aristo was the island from which the kingdom was ruled. It grew wealthy on its trade routes with Greece, Turkey and Egypt," Andreas said. "Calista had—*has*—its diamond mines. Pink diamonds. Very rare—but, of course, you know that."

Alex squeezed her hand in reassurance.

"The Karedes family—our family—got fat and rich trading those diamonds to Europe." He smiled wryly. "As you can probably imagine, the Calistans didn't like that. My grandfather—"

"King Christos," Maria said.

"Yes. He tried to alleviate the tension but it didn't work, so he announced that on his death, he'd leave Aristo to be ruled by my father and Calista to be ruled by my father's sister, Anya."

"And the people accepted that?"

"What else could they do?" Sebastian said. "But Christos always hoped for a reconciliation. Part of what he said, when he made his decision public, was that he wished the two halves of the Stefani diamond would someday be reunited and that when they were, the island would also be reunited as one nation, the nation of Adamas. We call it Christos's Legacy."

Kitty nodded. "But it hasn't happened."

"That must have been a difficult time for everyone." Maria looked at the king. "For you and your sister, especially, sir."

"It's all in the past," Aegeus snapped. "And I fail to see a need to go through it with a stranger." He tossed his napkin on the table. "You are to make a necklace for the queen, Ms. Santos, not write our family's history."

"Just a minute," Alex began, but Maria spoke first.

"My sole interest is in making the necklace as meaningful and perfect a gift as possible, sir." She sounded composed but Alex recognized that distinct, don't-screw-with-me lift of her chin. "I regret that you don't see it that way."

Alex bit back a grin. His Maria had been nervous about dining with royalty, but she sure as hell had the balls to stand up to Aegeus. His brothers were trying not to smile; his sister looked as if she might fly from her seat, grab Maria and kiss her. The queen gave a soft cough and covered her mouth with her napkin.

Aegeus looked as if he weren't sure if he'd been insulted or not. Finally he nodded, shoved back his chair and got to his feet.

The meal was over.

"Perhaps I overreacted, Ms. Santos. At any rate, a perfect gift is my wish, too. And now, if you require nothing further—"

"Actually," Maria said carefully, "actually, sir, I do."

Aegeus stared at her. So did the others. You could push the king just so far and then you had to stand back before the explosion.

"Do you, indeed?" he said coldly.

Maria looked determined but she was shaking. Enough, Alex decided, and, despite all the eyes on her, he moved closer and slipped his arm around her shoulders. At first, she stiffened. Then he felt her lean into him.

"It's—it's a request, sir." She took a deep breath. "I'd like to see the Aristan crown."

"You have seen it," the king said coolly. "My people provided you with photographs."

"Photos aren't the same as the real thing, Your Majesty."

"Impossible. For security purposes, the crown is kept in the royal vaults."

"Surely, it can be taken out of the vaults, Father," Alex said quietly.

"There is no need."

"Oh, but there is, sir," Maria said quickly. "I need to be certain the center diamond in the necklace, the big pink one, will be the correct shade. A diamond's true color can never be conveyed through a photo, no matter how good the photo is."

"You mentioned color in your proposal. That is the reason I provided you with two large pink stones rather than one." The king's lips twisted. "Surely you noticed that."

"Of course, Your Majesty. And I very much appreciate that thoughtful gesture."

"Thoughtful, and expensive, Ms. Santos."

"It was a generous thing to do, sir." Maria drew a breath. "But there are slight variations in the colors of the two pink diamonds. That's all the more reason for seeing the crown."

"I refer you, again, to the photographs. I have been assured that digital photos are quite accurate."

"Not when it comes to color," Maria said with quiet determination. "Plus, I need to see, to touch the Aristan half of the Stefani diamond." She flushed. "Stones have a way of speaking to those who work with them, sir. I know it may sound strange—"

"Strange?" Aegeus snorted. "It would seem I was correct in fearing this young woman might be a leftover flower child," he said to no one in particular, "instead of a jewelry maker."

"Actually, Father," Alex said coldly, "Maria is neither." He felt her body jerk against his. Deliberately, he drew her closer. "She is an artist, and we are very fortunate she agreed to create this piece." His eyes met Aegeus's. "I think you owe her an apology."

The king's face turned red. No one spoke for what seemed an eternity. Then the queen cleared her throat, stood and took her husband's arm.

"Aegeus, Alexandros. Please, let's not spoil the wonderful plans for my birthday celebration. I am so excited about this necklace... Just think, Aegeus, the entire world will be watching when you present it to me. The necklace should, indeed, be as perfect as Ms. Santos can make it, should it not? It should glow with the same light as the Aristan crown, especially since you'll be wearing the crown that night."

Silence. A muscle knotted in Alex's jaw. Then he nodded.

"Mother is right, Father. I'm sorry if I seemed rude, but I spoke the truth. Maria's talent will ensure that people everywhere will talk of Aristo, its crown and the queen's matching necklace for years to come."

The king stood as still as a statue. Then, at last, he jerked his head in assent.

"I'll make the arrangements. Ms. Santos, you shall have five minutes with the crown and the Stefani diamond. Five minutes, and not a second more. Is that clear?"

Maria stepped free of Alex's encircling arm and made a deep curtsy.

"It is, sir. And thank you. You won't regret your decision."

Aegeus looked at her. A shadow seemed to pass over his face.

"I hope not," he said, and strode away.

They drove back to the mansion in silence.

The gates swung open; the Ferrari purred down the long drive. When they reached the house, Alex turned off the engine, stepped from the car, opened Maria's door and thought what an amazing woman she was.

Bright. Talented. Strong.

And lovely.

Incredibly lovely, in the moonlight.

She would be even more lovely in his bed.

Naked. Her eyes on his as he undressed. Her arms reaching for him as he came to her and she *would* reach for him, he would find a way to make her admit how much she wanted him—and yet, at this moment, what he wanted most was to kiss away the worried furrow between her eyes, the sad little down-curve of her mouth.

He held out his hand. "We're home," he said softly.

She nodded, took his hand and stepped from the car.

"Your father will probably send me back to the States tomorrow."

Alex smiled. "No danger of that," he said as they walked to the door. "He's trapped. My mother, clever woman that she is, reminded him that the world will be watching when she celebrates her birthday."

"Don't try and make it sound as if I didn't behave foolishly!"

"The word I'd use is 'bravely.'"

"I don't know what got into me. It's just—"

"What got into you," he said, turning her to him, "was all that fiery passion you do your best to hide."

"I don't hide anything. I just—"

"And you do a pretty good job of it—until something comes along and heats your blood." He opened the door to the sleeping house, then turned toward her again and caught a cluster of silky curls in his fingers. "Tonight, it was the ridiculous behavior of a king."

"No. I mean, I only—"

"And your dedication to your art."

"That's—that's nice of you to say, but I made everyone uncomfortable——"

"And me." His voice roughened. He cupped the nape of her neck, slipped his fingers into her hair and tilted her face to his. "I heat your blood, *agapimeni*. As you heat mine."

He bent his head and kissed her. It was a gentle kiss, the soft whisper of his lips over hers, but it made him groan.

"Maria," he said softly, and he felt her tremble. "Maria," he said again, and her arms rose, wound around his neck; she lifted herself to him, sighed his name and when he kissed her again he went deep. Deeper, letting the taste of her fill his senses, the feel of her feed his soul...

And he knew, without question, that he could not, would not hold her to the devil's bargain they'd made.

Gently, he cupped her face and drew back. Her eyes opened slowly; she looked up at him, her pupils dark and wide and blurred with desire or perhaps with tears. It killed him that he couldn't tell the difference.

"It's late," he said. "Too late to discuss this tonight." His gaze fell to her lips. He longed to kiss her again but he wouldn't. He wouldn't. He wouldn't. "Can you find your way to your bedroom alone?"

"But I thought— You said—"

"I know what I said." He drew a ragged breath and then, to hell with it, he kissed her. "I'm not a saint, Maria," he whispered against her mouth, "but it turns out that I'm not quite the bastard we both thought."

A sound that might have been a sob broke from her throat. "I don't understand, Alexandros. What is it you want from me?"

He shook his head, left her standing alone as he headed out into the night.

He didn't know what he wanted from her.

And that was the whole damned problem.

CHAPTER NINE

WHAT did a man do when he was obviously losing his sanity?

It had to be that because he sure as hell wasn't into martyrdom, Alex thought as he paced through the dark garden. Maybe he deserved a medal. Better still, maybe he should get his head checked by a shrink because right now, *right now*, instead of burning with frustration, he could be bedding the woman he'd brought across an ocean for expressly that purpose.

Maria had been his. His for the taking.

And he'd walked away.

"Idiot," he said, kicking a stone out of the path.

Walked away, and for what reason? She'd been as ready for sex as he was. She wasn't an innocent. Nothing he'd have done would have shocked her.

Alex glared at the house where a light still burned in his bedroom window. He could be in the house, in that room in less than a minute.

Forget it.

He'd made his decision. For tonight, anyway. Going back would be an admission of weakness, never mind that he didn't really know what in hell he meant by that, except that he knew it would be.

He needed sex, not Maria. That put things in perspective.

He was aroused. No problem. There were ways to deal with it. Phone one of the numbers programmed into his cell phone. There were half a dozen beautiful women who'd jump at the chance to spend the night with him. Or he could drive back into town. The bar at The Grand Hotel saw more than its share of gorgeous women, tourists hoping for a little adventure.

Except, he didn't want another woman, and wasn't that a laugh? He wanted Maria and he'd just walked away from her.

Alex kicked another stone and headed for his Ferrari.

He roared out of the gates, took the coast road at a speed that sent him flying past the few startled drivers on the road at this late hour. When he reached the point at which the already narrow, winding road grew more treacherous, he floored the gas pedal and the car careered through the turns like the thoroughbred it was.

Maybe that would burn away the hunger thrumming through his blood.

It didn't.

Two hours later, he pulled through the gates of the mansion again and skidded to a stop with Maria still in his head. Images. Memories. Tastes and scents, all of them conspiring against him. The softness of her skin. The honey of her mouth. The texture of her uptilted nipples on his tongue. The scent of her desire.

She was there, in his brain, and nothing could dislodge her.

Well, yeah. One thing could.

His body hardened like a fist.

Having her would do it. Stripping off her clothes. Baring her body to his eyes. To his hands. His mouth. Clasping her wrists, holding them high over her head so she had no choice but to let him touch her everywhere until she wept with wanting him.

Then he'd sink into her. Deep, deep into her. He'd move inside her until she screamed his name, until she came and came and came…

A growl of anger, of desire, of something close to lunacy rose in his throat. He crossed his hands on the steering wheel and slammed his forehead against them. After a few minutes, he stepped from the car and entered the house.

It was quiet. Dark. The furniture cast ominous black shadows against the walls.

Alex's mouth thinned as he stood in the entry foyer and stared up at the second floor landing.

He was no knight in shining armor. He was a man who had grown up in a world of privilege, a man who could have what he wanted when he wanted it. Especially women. The more beautiful they were, the more famous, the more they threw themselves at his feet. They begged for his possession. Preened to ready themselves for his taking, not like Maria who asked nothing of him and had packed a suitcase full of jeans to wear in her role as his mistress.

She looked beautiful in jeans.

And in that dress tonight, those sexy shoes, stuff he'd ordered over the phone just figuring anything the color of emeralds would be perfect against her dark hair and eyes…

When she'd opened that door, when he saw her… God, he'd wanted to push her back inside the room, tumble her on the bed, make love to her until she had no choice but to admit she'd dreamed of this, ached for this, that she wanted him, only him…

He swung away from the staircase, marched through the silent house to his study, poured himself a shot of brandy, slugged it down and did what he'd been doing hours ago in the garden, paced and paced and paced.

A sto diavolo! The hell with it! He was weary of the game. It was time to end it.

He took the stairs two at a time, went down the hall, stopped before the door to his bedroom, raised his fist to knock... Knock? At his own damned door? Bad enough he'd showered and dressed in his study, that he'd spent the last couple of hours driving aimlessly through the night. He cursed, ripely and creatively, grabbed the knob and turned it, ready to break the damned door down if he had to.

It opened easily.

Maria wasn't there. The emerald dress was crumpled on a chair, the black stilettos were on the floor next to it.

The bed was untouched.

His anger vanished. Fear took its place. Where was she? Had she left? Not likely. She'd have had to phone for a taxi, and a cab would not have been able to clear the gates without alerting Security.

What, then? Had she gone for a walk ? Alex's

mouth tightened. She wouldn't have done that, would she? Not at night. Not when she didn't know the complex layout of the gardens, the density of the surrounding trees.

The way some of the pathways ended at vistas at the very edge of the cliff.

No, he thought, forcing aside the ugly possibility. If she were wandering the grounds, motion detectors would have picked her up. Then where…?

The guesthouse!

Alex pounded down the stairs and out the door, walking fast, running, really, his anger back and hotter than ever. Did she think she could escape him? That he'd let her sleep there rather than in his bed, where she belonged? Yes. There was a faint light shining in the guesthouse window.

"Damn it, Maria," he growled as he flung open the door, "if you think I'm going to go on being a Boy Scout…"

The furious words died on his tongue.

She was huddled in a window seat, illuminated by the flickering glow of candlelight. She wore jeans and an oversized sweatshirt, her feet were tucked up under her and when she heard his voice, she swung toward him, face pale, eyes huge and stricken and glittering with tears.

"I'm sorry," she said in a broken whisper. "I'm sorry for everything, Alexandros. I should never have come here. I know what I agreed to but I can't do it, I can't, I can't."

By then, he'd crossed the space between them and gathered her into his arms.

"Don't," she said.

He ignored the plea, whispered to her in Greek the way he might have whispered to a terrified child. He stroked her hair, rocked her against him and she began to sob.

"I know I agreed to—to be your mistress, but I can't do it. Even if it means losing the commission. I can't. I can't. I really thought I could but—"

"No. Of course, you can't." He drew her into his lap. "Shh, *glyka mou.* I won't hurt you. I could never hurt you. Please, don't cry."

"I didn't know who you were that night, Alexandros. I swear it. I went with you because—because…I can't explain it. I'd never done anything like that before. I'd never even—I'd never even—" She drew a ragged breath. "I know you won't believe me but—but I'd never been with a man before."

Ah, dear Lord!

The sweet, sad little confession made him feel like a bastard—and filled him with joy. He *did* believe her; the truth was, he'd known it, deep within himself, all along. His beautiful Maria had given him her innocence. Hell, he had taken it from her. And, of course, she had not known who he was.

She was incapable of that kind of subterfuge. Why hadn't he belicved her? How could he have been so stupid? How could he have judged her by what he knew of other women, the ones who'd tried to trap him with their lies? There had been so many of them, starting with the Greek girl who'd broken his heart when they'd both been kids. He'd been sure he loved her and when she wept and trembled and told him he'd stolen her virginity, he'd been ready to marry her— until he'd caught her laughing with her friends at his gullibility. The Italian debutante who said she'd die in sin if he didn't take her as his wife, except it turned out she'd already slept with half the young princes in Europe. The German super-model who'd accused him of making her pregnant. Wiser than in the past, he'd demanded a paternity test—and had not heard from her again.

But Maria was nothing like that. She was—she was Maria, sweet and smart and brave, and he'd put her through hell.

"I'll recommend someone good, someone excellent to take my place making the necklace," she said in a low voice . "You can let him use my design—I owe your mother that—but—"

Alex stopped the flow of words with a soft kiss.

"You owe no one anything, *glyka mou*. And why would I let someone take your place?" Smiling, he thumbed a strand of dark hair from her brow. "There is no one who could replace you, sweetheart. Like your design, you are one of a kind."

"But I just told you, I can't—"

"Maria." He framed her face with his hands. "I'm setting you free of our agreement. You'll stay here, create a necklace the entire world will admire—but not because we've made love." He took a deep breath. "I want you, *kardia mou*. I want you so much it hurts. But I would never take something you would not willingly give." His mouth twisted. "I did that to you once, and I will never forgive myself for—"

She put her fingers lightly over his mouth.

"I gave myself to you that night, Alex. I wanted you." She swallowed, ran the tip of her tongue over her bottom lip. "I want you now."

Could a woman's soft words make the

universe tilt? "Sweetheart. Do you know what you're saying?"

She gave a watery little laugh. "I know exactly what I'm saying. That's why I can't stay here. I want you, despite what you think of me, and isn't that terrible? To admit something that—that strips me of what little pride I have left—"

He kissed her. "Hush," he whispered.

"It's the truth. If I had any pride, I wouldn't have come to Aristo with you. I wouldn't have said I'd sleep with you. Because—because it wasn't only the commission, Alex, it was being with you…"

He kissed her again. He meant the kiss to be gentle and that was how it began but somehow her lips parted under his. The tip of her tongue slipped into his mouth. And when she wound her arms around his neck and dragged his face down to hers, he reached blindly for one final bit of sanity.

"Maria," he said against her mouth, "sweetheart, be sure. Be very sure—"

"I've never been more sure of anything in my life."

Alex groaned, swept her into his arms and carried her through the moonlight to the bed.

This bed was not like his.

It was smaller. Simpler. It had been made from

a centuries-old olive tree and was covered in white cotton loomed in a nearby village. It had an intrinsic, natural beauty all its own.

It was, Alex thought as he lay Maria across it, beautiful in the same way as she, with a quiet strength and an elegance that came from within.

"Alexandros," she sighed, and raised her arms to him.

He went into her embrace and kissed her.

Two months ago, a lifetime ago, they had made love fiercely. He had all but torn off her clothes in his frenzy to bury himself inside her.

That had been sex.

Now…now, it was something more.

He kissed her again and again, until her lips were as soft as rose petals and clung hungrily to his. He framed her face, threaded his fingers into her hair, kissed her throat, nipped at the tender flesh at the juncture of neck and shoulder and when she moaned with pleasure, he could have sworn he felt his heart lift in his chest.

Slowly, he sat her up. Drew her sweatshirt over her head and discovered, to his delight, that she wore nothing beneath it or the jeans that he tossed aside.

Naked, she was a moon-kissed offering to the gods.

Beautiful. Perfect. Exquisitely feminine.

Slowly, so slowly, his eyes on hers, he stroked the contours of her body. Her breasts. Her belly. Her thighs. She sighed and moaned and made the kinds of little sounds that told him, as much as the sensual lift of her hips, that what he was doing pleased her.

Still, he had to ask.

"Do you like this?" he whispered, sucking a beaded nipple deep into the heat of his mouth. "This?" he said, kissing his way from breast to belly. "This?" he said softly, dropping a kiss on the soft curls at the juncture of her thighs.

"Alexandros," she said, "oh God, Alexandros…"

Gently, he parted her thighs. Put his hands under her bottom. Lifted her to him, put his mouth to the delicate cleft of her flesh, found her with his mouth, his tongue, and her scream of joy shattered the night.

It was almost too much for him.

He was so close to the edge. All these weeks of wanting her. And, though it seemed crazy, all the years of wanting her, as well.

"Alexandros," she whispered, and he kissed her mouth, her throat and knew that he, like Paris when he stole Helen centuries before, had not been able to obey the rules of the civilized world.

This was what he had wanted, this woman, this lover, and he had done whatever it took to have her.

He would have given everything for this, the honeyed taste of her mouth. This, the sweetness of her nipples. This, the indentation of her navel. This, the curve of her hips.

This, he thought, just this, holding her, tasting her, watching her face as he caressed her. As he again parted the delicate petals that protected her clitoris.

He kissed her there again. Licked her until she came again. This time, when she cried out, she reached for him.

"Please, Alexandros," she said, "please. Come into me."

Quickly, he tore off his clothes. Came back to her, swore, reached for his discarded jacket, dug into the inside pocket and prayed he'd find a condom. He did, and he tore the little packet open, rolled the condom on. He'd forgotten to use one the first time he'd made love to her; he'd been too hungry, too out of control.

He was almost out of control now. That was what happened to him, when he was with her.

He moved up her body, took her in his arms, kissed her, let her taste the proof of their passion in his kiss. Her hands were on him now, cool against his skin. She stroked her palms along his shoulders, his chest, down his belly and when one hand moved lower and almost closed around his hard length, his breath hissed between his teeth.

"Maria," he said in a warning whisper. "Maria, *glyka mou…*"

She caressed him anyway, her hand moving, moving up and down over his swollen sex, and he groaned, caught her hand and stilled it and knew he could wait no longer.

"Look at me, *agapi mou.* Watch me as I make you mine."

Her lashes lifted. Her eyes met his. He clasped both her hands. Laced their fingers together. Held their hands to the sides and thrust into her.

She came instantly, her body arching to his, her cries of abandon rising into the night and still he eased forward. Deeper. Deeper until there was no way to know where he began and she ended, until their flesh, their souls, were one.

"Maria," he said, "Maria, *kardia mou, agapi mou…*"

She wept and kissed his mouth, and as the muscles of her womb contracted rhythmically around him, Alexandros threw back his head and emptied himself into the sweet warmth of the woman who now belonged to him.

To me, he thought fiercely. *Only to me.*

CHAPTER TEN

FOR a long moment, the world stood still.

Alex's powerful body was sprawled over Maria's, his face buried in her throat, their hearts still racing, skin damp with the commingled sweat of their passion. The night breeze, drifting across them from the still-open door, was chill. But when Alex began to ease away, Maria tightened her arms around him.

"Don't go," she murmured, and felt his lips curve in a smile.

"I'm not going very far."

He reached for the throw at the foot of the bed, wrapped it around them, rolled to his side and gathered her close in his arms.

"Are you all right?"

It was her turn to smile. "Yes."

"You sure?""

"Very sure. I'm fine. I'm perfect. I'm—"

"Yes," he said, laughing softly as he kissed her, "you are." Tenderly, he brushed back the tangled curls on her forehead. "Forgive me, *agapi mou*."

"For what?"

"For not making love to you this way the first time."

She shook her head, lay her hand against his cheek. "That first time was wonderful."

A very male smile lit his face. "Thank you. But you were a virgin. I should have gone slower."

"You didn't know."

"I should have." He turned his face into her hand and kissed the palm. "There was such a sweetness to you, *glyka mou*. Such an innocence. The way you touched me. Responded to me." His hand slipped down her body, cupping her breast, then the curve of her hip. "I've relived those moments a hundred times," he said huskily. "The feel of you. Your little cries. The way you blushed when I undressed you." His mouth twisted. "The way I ruined it all with my terrible accusations."

Maria put a finger over his lips. "Didn't some wise man once say that the past is best left in the past?"

Alex drew her fingertip into the heat of his mouth. "Do you forgive me?"

"Forgive you for what?" she said, with a little

smile. "I don't know what you're talking about, Alexandros."

His eyes darkened. "I love how you say my name."

"Alexandros," she sighed, "Alexandros, Alexandros, Alexandros…"

Just that—the sound of her voice, the feel of her against him—and he felt himself turning hard. "Maria," he said, "my Maria," and then he was inside her again, deep inside her, and the night enfolded them in its magical embrace.

Just before sunrise, when the grass glittered with dew, they dressed and made their way to the house.

"Someone will see us," Maria hissed as Alex drew her inside.

"Who could possibly see us?"

"Spoken like a true potentate," she said, laughing up at him. "What about Athenia? The cook? The maids? The rest of the staff?"

Alex swung her into his arms and carried her to his room. "The souls of discretion, I promise."

Well, of course. They would be. Maria's smile dimmed just a little. No point in being foolish about this. Other women would have slept in Alex's bed…

"No."

She looked up. Alex was watching her and smiling.

"No, what?"

"No other women, sweetheart. Not here." He could see that she was surprised. And pleased. Crazy as it seemed, so was he. He set her on her feet, gently pushed her back against the closed bedroom door and framed her face with his hands. "Just you. Which means," he said solemnly, but with a glint of laughter in his eyes, "we're going to have to celebrate the occasion. Initiate my bed properly." He bent his head, brushed her lips with his. "Champagne. Candles. Rose petals. How does that sound?"

Could he feel her heart racing? Could he possibly know what was in that racing heart, the emotions that she had spent the past two months, the past two days trying her best to deny?

"It sounds wonderful." She moved, just a little, enough so she was pressed against him. "But won't it take an awfully long time to get all those things together?"

She saw the change sweep through him. The narrowed mouth. The tic of a muscle in his jaw. The hint of exciting male passion that seemed to make the beautiful structure of his face even more pronounced.

"Maria," he said thickly, "Dear God, Maria…"

They didn't make it to the bed. Not then. But they did the next time, and the next, where they made love until the Aristan sun blazed bright and hot in the perfect blue of the sky.

When he awoke, the space beside him was empty. He sat up, the covers falling to his waist.

"Maria?" Naked, he padded to the bathroom. The door was locked; he heard the sound of running water and then nothing. "Maria?" he said again, and knocked.

"I'm fine," she called, but the weak sound of her voice was evidence of the lie. His heart turned over. She'd been sick before, sick again, and now… "Maria? Open the door. Please."

There was a silence. Then he heard the lock turn. The door swung open and he saw his Maria, standing at the sink with a toothbrush in her hand, looking at him in the mirror. She smiled, but her face was pale and sweaty.

"*Kardia mou,*" Alex said urgently, stepping behind her and encircling her with his arms, "were you ill again?"

She nodded. "A little."

"Maria, this has happened too often."

"It's just flu, Alexandros," she said, forcing another smile. "New York's loaded with it."

"This is not flu. I had flu last winter. Andreas had it, too. With flu you're sick and then you get better. But you—you're not getting better."

"I am. Much better."

"I will take you to my doctor."

"Don't be silly."

"He will examine you, *glyka mou*, and prescribe an antibiotic."

"Antibiotics don't work against viruses, and flu is a virus."

"Such logic," Alex said, trying to sound angry when what he felt was fear. She was so pale, her eyes so dark… "Come here," he said, and turned her and drew her close. "I don't want you to be sick, sweetheart. Let me take care of you."

"I'm fine. Honestly."

"*Thee mou*, you're a stubborn woman! Very well. No doctor." He swung her up in his arms. "At least, come back to bed and rest for a little while."

He carried her to the bed and lay down with her in his arms. Kissed her tenderly. Stroked her back. And, inevitably, as he held her, as his body heated hers, as she burrowed against him, tenderness gave way to desire.

"Are you sure you're okay?" he whispered as he touched her. "Shall I stop?"

"Don't stop," she whispered back, "don't ever stop."

And he didn't.

She was gone again, the next time he awoke.

A knot of apprehension formed in his belly but the bathroom door stood open and the room was empty.

He showered quickly, pulled on jeans, a white T-shirt and mocs, and went downstairs. He could hear the radio playing softly in the kitchen, turned to Athenia's favorite music station. She smiled at him.

"*Kalimera*, sir."

"Have you seen Miss Santos?"

"Oh, yes, perhaps an hour ago. She had coffee and—"

"She was all right?"

His housekeeper raised her eyebrows. "Fine, sir. She went to the guesthouse. To her workshop, I mean."

The workshop. Alex ran a hand through his hair. "Of course," he said sheepishly.

He found her there, perched on a high stool

at a workbench. She was wearing jeans and a blue chambray shirt with the sleeves rolled up. She'd pulled her hair back in a ponytail; her feet were bare, one on the rung of the stool, one on the floor. She was bent over a sketch-pad, intensity in every line of her body, and humming something he couldn't identify other than to be sure the tune was almost painfully off-key.

He smiled, came up behind her quietly and slipped his arms around her.

"*Kalimera, kardoula mou,*" he said softly, and kissed the nape of her neck.

She sank back against him, her head against his shoulder, her hands covering his.

"*Kalimera, Alexandros,*" she said, and turned her face to his for a kiss.

"Mmm," he said. She tasted wonderful, of coffee and of herself. "I missed you."

She laughed. "I'm glad to hear it."

Alex grinned and turned her in his arms. "Then, why were you in such a hurry to leave my bed?"

"Oh, I wasn't in a hurry at all!" She blushed. "I mean—"

"Such a nice compliment, *glyka mou*. No need to explain it away."

Maria linked her hands behind his neck. "I woke up and thought of a small change I want to make in your mother's necklace. Nothing that will alter the design," she said hastily, "just a modification in the way I planned to position the central stone. I promise, she'll still like it."

"She'll love it, Maria. She thinks the design, your work, all the pictures you sent, are brilliant."

Her face glowed with pleasure. "I'm so glad, Alexandros! This commission means the world to me."

His gaze fell to her lips. "What else means the world to you?" he said huskily.

His hands slid under her shirt, cupped her breasts. Her breath caught; he watched her eyes turn from hazel to coffee-brown to ink-black.

"This," she said, covering his hands with hers, "oh, this, this, this…"

He carried her to the bed. And as he came down beside her and kissed her, as they undressed each other, as she kissed his mouth, his throat, his chest, his belly and, at last, touched the tip of her tongue to the silk-over-steel power of his erection, she knew that what she'd just told him was only partly true.

This—touching him, kissing him, sharing his

passion—did mean the world, but only because—because…

Because she loved him.

They had brunch, what Athenia referred to as a *kolatsio*, a snack, on a terrace overlooking the water. Thick, sweet Greek coffee. Olives. Feta cheese. Slices of warm, delicious bread and a tray of sweet cheese pastries that Alex said were called *kalitsounia kritis*.

They should have been called heavenly. The pastries were delicious and decadent and surely fattening but Maria didn't care. She would not worry about anything this morning, not when life was so perfect. Even the day was perfect. Bright. Sunny. Warm. Unusual for the time of year, Alexandros said, and nothing like the weather they'd left behind in New York.

The truth was, nothing was like what she'd left in New York. Not this beautiful place. And not this wonderful, gorgeous, sexy, strong, funny, caring, intelligent man.

Now, Maria, Sister Sarah would have cautioned, *that's far too many adjectives.*

Yes, Maria thought, but Sister had never met Alex.

He was seated across from her, talking about his

house. He loved it; she could see that in his animated face. He was proud of it; she could hear that in his voice. How did you come to find such a perfect house? she'd asked, and he'd said, with a boyish grin, that he hadn't found it, he'd built it.

And he had.

He'd worked along with the architect. With the builder. With the carpenters. He'd wanted a house that blended into its surroundings, that was spare and strong and unique.

"Like these cliffs," he said.

Like you, she thought.

He told her that he'd lived in the palace until he'd gone away to boarding school and then university, and, though he loved its history and elegance, it had never felt like home. So, once he had his MBA, he'd bought a condo in Ellos and another in New York. Then, one weekend at the family compound overlooking the turbulent waters that separated Aristo and Calista, the Strait of Poseidon that Kitty had mentioned at dinner, it had suddenly hit him that what he wanted was a place of his own, overlooking the sea.

"I'd always loved driving along these cliffs so it seemed natural to call a friend, a realtor, inquire about property, then bring another friend, an architect, to see what he might suggest, and—"

Alex laughed. "Look at you, *kardoula mou*. Your beautiful eyes are glazing over, thanks to my endless talk about myself." He reached for her hands, lifted them to his lips and kissed them. "What I really want to talk about is you."

She smiled. "My life isn't anywhere near as interesting. And my eyes aren't glazing over. I love learning things about you, Alexandros."

She did. Oh, she did! She'd gone from hating him to loving him in what seemed a heartbeat but the truth was, she'd fallen in love with him that first terrible night.

"Still, I won't say another word until you tell me about Maria Santos."

"It's a dull— Hey," she said, laughing as Alex, in one fast move, rose from his chair, tugged her into his arms and settled into his chair again but this time with her in his lap.

"Okay, then," he said, "I'll tell you about her. Maria Santos was born twenty-five years ago. She was the most beautiful baby anyone had ever seen."

Maria began to laugh. "Alex, that's silly!"

"What?" he said, his eyes round with innocence. "You mean, you're not twenty-five? What are you, then? Forty-five? Fifty-five? My God, you can't be sixty—"

"I was not the most beautiful baby anyone had ever seen."

"I'll bet you were."

"I was premature. Tiny. Skinny. Almost bald."

"Beautiful," Alex said, grinning, "just as I said."

Maria rolled her eyes. "You're crazy, Alexandros."

"Crazy about you," he said softly.

Could your heart really sing? She'd never heard such thrilling words. Her prince. Her lover. Her Alexandros was crazy about her.

"And I want to know all about you."

That was wonderful, too. No one had ever wanted to know all about her, not once in her entire life. Smiling, she pressed her lips lightly to his.

"Okay," she said softly, "here's the entire, unexciting tale. I was born in the Bronx. I went to school in the Bronx. Public elementary and middle schools, and high school at Saint Mary's. Then I went to college in—"

"The Bronx?" Alex said, and smiled.

"You guessed it. Lehman College. I studied—"

"Art."

She sighed and lay her head against his shoulder. "I studied business. Mama's idea, and I hated it. When everybody was studying Word and Excel, I sketched. Back then, before I discovered I loved working with metal and stones, I thought I wanted to design clothes. Anyway, I stuck it out for a year. Then I did what I had to do. I worked up a portfolio, arranged for an interview at FIT—the Fashion Institute of Technology. They accepted me, I made all the arrangements for a student loan." She took a breath. "Then I broke the news to Mama. I told her how hard it was to get into FIT, I showed her my portfolio, and she said—"

"She said you had amazing talent, and that you'd be the next—who's that New York designer? Donna Karan?"

Maria smiled, but her smile trembled. "She said I was a foolish girl with silly dreams."

Alex's arms tightened around her. "Ah, sweetheart, I'm sorry. I should have figured…I mean, the other night—"

"No, it's okay. Maybe it'll help you understand why—why she acted the way she did when you met her." She took a deep breath. "See, my mother never finished high school. She went to work when she was sixteen, operating a sewing machine in the garment center. She was determined I would not do the same, and I couldn't make her see that I wouldn't end up that way."

"And your father?"

"What about him?" she said, with a nonchalance as transparent as glass. "He owned the company where Mama worked. He was rich. He had a house on Long Island. He had a big car." She cleared her throat. "He also had a wife and kids."

"And your poor mother had no idea…" Alex said tightly.

"She had every idea." Maria's voice turned brittle. "He said he'd leave his wife and marry her—but, of course, he didn't. And then, when she told him she was pregnant with me, he said she was lying. When he realized it was the truth, he gave her some money. For an abortion, he said. But she didn't have an abortion, she had me instead, and he said that had been her decision, a bad decision, and then he fired her and she never saw him again."

Alex had gone very still. Maria bit back a groan. Whatever had possessed her to tell him all that? She could have just told him the first part. School. College. FIT. But the rest…Why had she unloaded that sad, dumb story on him? She never talked about her life. Never. Joaquin knew, but they'd grown up together. Sela knew, but she was her best friend. No one else knew that she was a bastard and yes, that was the right word. It was an old-fashioned word in lots of places but in Maria's world, the world her mother had created and in which she had raised her, the word still carried the smear of disgrace and dishonor.

Stupid, she told herself fiercely, *how incredibly stupid, to tell such ugly things to a man who might as well have been born and raised on another planet.*

"Well," she said brightly, "so much for Tales from the Bronx." She sat forward in Alex's lap. "This has been a lovely break, Alex, but I have to get to work and—"

"Has he never tried to see you?"

"Who?" she said, even more brightly. "Oh, my father? No. Why would he? I didn't need anything from him. I wouldn't take anything, even if he—"

"How could a man turn his back on the woman who carried his child? On the child herself?"

"Well, I don't know, but—"

Alex turned her face to his, cupped it with his hands and kissed her.

"You're a strong, brave woman, *kardia mou,*" he said softly. "And I am honored to have become your lover."

* * *

They fell into an easy pattern, like lovers who had been together a long time.

Not that what happened in bed lost its excitement.

It couldn't, not when the sight of Alex coming toward her sent Maria's pulse skittering, not when Maria's smile was enough to fill Alex with such hunger that there were times he had to turn away to keep from sweeping her into his arms and making love to her wherever they happened to be.

He didn't always turn away.

He made love to her in the workshop. In the garden. In the back of the limo with the privacy screen up, bringing her to climax with his hand high under her skirt, his mouth hot on hers. And he made love to her in bed. The demure bed in the workshop; the big, beautiful one in his room. They made love, and talked and laughed, and worked—she in her workshop, he in his study at the house. And they discovered all the things they needed to know about each other.

Maria no longer felt ill. The early morning nausea was a thing of the past. There were times she still felt exhausted but flu often left you feeling tired; everyone said so.

The only dark moments came when she remembered that her days with Alex were slipping away. The necklace was almost finished, the big birthday celebration loomed on the horizon. A week passed, then another, and the final week of her stay began.

When it ended, there would be nothing to keep her here.

Unless Alex asked her to stay. And she, who had spent her life avoiding relationships, who had never imagined repeating her mother's foolish involvement with a man who was all wrong for her...

She knew she would stay, if Alexandros asked her.

But he didn't. Why would he? *How* would he? He was a prince while she—she was a girl born into illegitimacy and raised in poverty. She could have a place in Alex's bed but she would never have one in his life.

So she concentrated on completing the necklace until, finally, she had only to set one of the fabulous pink stones in its center, but she had to see the Crown of Aristo before she could do that.

The king kept making appointments for that to happen, then cancelling them.

On a rainy afternoon just days before the queen's birthday party, Maria decided this couldn't go on. Alex had a meeting in Ellos. After he was gone, she phoned the palace, left a polite message with Aegeus's personal secretary. She had to see the crown today, she said, or the queen's gift might not be as perfect as the king and she both wished.

She hung up the phone and was suddenly overwhelmed by nausea. It took her by surprise. Apparently, she wasn't over the flu quite yet.

She barely made it to the bathroom, where she was horribly sick.

When the spasms finally ended, she flushed the toilet, brushed her teeth, rinsed her mouth and started for the bedroom when a shocking wave of vertigo swept over her.

Maria stumbled and fell against the door jamb. The collision wasn't particularly hard but the impact was painful and hurt her breasts. They'd grown so tender lately; even making love with Alex, there were times the touch of his mouth on her nipples came close to being painful…

Oh God!

Tender breasts. Nausea that seemed to have no basis. And, she thought, biting back a moan, and a period that had not come in…in, what? Two months? Three?

"No," she whispered, "please, please, no…"

The phone rang. She tried to ignore it but the ringing went on and on…

"Hello?"

It was the king's secretary. She would be permitted to see the crown an hour from now.

"I can't," Maria said, trembling as she counted back, again and again, to the last time she'd menstruated. "How about this afternoon? Or this evening?"

"One hour, Ms. Santos," a commanding voice barked through the phone, "or not at all."

It was the king himself, and she knew he meant it.

"I'll be there, Your Majesty," she whispered.

She—and the illegitimate royal baby she now realized lay cradled in her womb.

CHAPTER ELEVEN

MARIA showered quickly and dried her hair while trying not to think about anything but the meeting with the king…

Impossible, she thought as she dropped onto the edge of the bed.

How could she be pregnant? Alex had used condoms every time they'd made love. Well, not the very first time, almost three months ago. Things had happened so quickly that night…

After, he'd said, "You have the right to know that I have no diseases," and she, embarrassed by the conversation, had thought of telling him that she couldn't possibly have any because she'd never been with a man until him, but it had been easier to say that she had none, either.

"I assume you're on the pill," he'd added.

Well, of course, she wasn't. But it had been the safe time of her cycle so she'd just nodded instead of answering and left it at that.

Maria groaned and buried her face in her

hands. She thought of all the times she'd silently wondered how her mother could have made so many devastating mistakes. Now, she knew one answer was that making mistakes when you were swept away by passion was pathetically easy.

And all the signs she'd ignored! Nausea. Wooziness. Exhaustion. Not getting her period. That should have been the most damning evidence of all, but she'd never been completely regular...

Maybe you didn't see what you didn't want to see. Maybe it was just that simple.

She wanted to weep. To scream. To bang her fists against the wall. That she, of all women, should have tumbled into the age-old trap...

She knotted her hands in her lap. Took deep, calming breaths. Hysteria wouldn't change anything. Besides, there was no time for this now. The necklace. The summons from the king. Those things came first. She had responsibilities. To the queen. To herself.

She dressed quickly. Black trousers, a black cashmere sweater and, over it, a pale pink jacket. Black heels. Alex had followed his gift of the emerald silk dress with what seemed like an endless wardrobe, ordered from the pricey designer boutiques in Ellos and delivered to the mansion.

"I can't let you buy me things like this," she'd protested, and he'd kissed her to silence.

"I love giving you gifts, *agapi mou*," he'd said, and because she'd known he meant it, because nothing had turned out as she'd anticipated and instead of only being in Alex's bed she was also in his life, she'd accepted the clothes and wore them when they went out to dinner, to the theater, to the casino.

Now, the rack of expensive outfits in the dressing room—*his* dressing room—was a mocking reminder that these were not simply gifts, they were proof she was his mistress.

And mistresses did not get pregnant. They did not have babies. They did not forge real, lasting relationships that led to a joint future, especially with a man like Alex. A prince of the Royal House of Karedes…

"Stop it," she said sharply, and blanked her mind to everything but the meeting with King Aegeus. She had worked years for this kind of professional honor.

Right now, that was all that mattered.

* * *

Weeks before, Alex had arranged for his limo to be at her disposal.

"Don't trust me to drive, hmm?" she'd said, laughing.

"Not on these roads, *glyka mou*," he'd said, and she'd admitted that was for the best. A born and bred New Yorker, she'd learned to drive but she didn't do it often or well.

Today would most certainly not have been a day to test her skill.

The driver had apparently been told where to take her. He drove through the palace gates to a rear courtyard where an equerry greeted her and led her through a maze of corridors to a half-opened door in a gloomy alcove.

"Ms. Santos, sir."

The king was seated at a small table, a velvet drawstring bag before him. A chair was drawn up opposite his. Maria blinked. Were these the royal vaults? She'd expected something different. Bright lights. Security cameras. Guards. Not a small, plain, ill-lit room.

"Your Majesty," she began, but Aegeus cut her off with an imperious wave. Another wave dismissed the equerry. Aegeus pointed at the other chair.

"Ms. Santos. Sit down."

His tone was hard, a direct contrast to his looks. She was surprised by his pallor and the throb of a vein in his forehead.

"Are you—are you all right, sir?"

Aegeus glared at her. "Are you a physician as well as my son's mistress? Oh, don't look so shocked, Ms. Santos. I'm not a fool. I am aware of everything that happens in my kingdom."

"Then you are aware that I'm here as the designer of Queen Tia's birthday gift, sir, nothing else."

She knew she'd overstepped the boundary between commoner and king but the last thing she would let happen today was a discussion of her relationship with Alex.

To her surprise, Aegeus laughed. "I can understand Alex's infatuation. A woman with beauty and intelligence and spirit..." His smile tilted. "What man could resist such temptation?"

Maria drew a deep breath. "Your Majesty. The crown..."

Aegeus pushed the velvet bag into the center of the table but kept his hand protectively on it.

"Normally, it is kept in a display case along with the Crown Jewels and, of course, the original Crown of Adamas."

"Yes, sir. To tell the truth, I'm surprised that—"

"Your surprise does not interest me, Ms. Santos. I've arranged to meet you here so we could keep things as simple and private as possible." He raised his wrist, pointedly looked at his watch and then at her. "Five minutes. Then your time is up."

Maria nodded and reached for the bag. The vein in the king's forehead seemed to leap as he lifted his hand and sat back.

She loosened the drawstring and lifted the Crown of Aristo from it.

Her breath caught. The crown was magnificent.

Brilliant white diamonds shone like star fire even in the dim light. Yes, she thought happily, yes, they'd match the ones in the necklace perfectly, but it was the fantastic center stone that dazzled the eye. The half of the pure pink Stefani diamond King Christos had bequeathed to his son, Aegeus, and to the kingdom of Aristo, dominated the crown.

"Beautiful," Maria said softly.

Aegeus nodded. "Yes," he said brusquely, and reached for the crown.

"Wait," Maria said quickly, pulling it back.

He looked up. The vein in his forehead looked

even darker than before. "You forget yourself, Ms. Santos."

"I meant…Wait. Please, Your Majesty."

"For what? You've seen what you came to see."

"I want a closer look at the pink diamond, sir. To check its shade against…" Maria took a small silk bag from the leather tote she always carried when handling gems. She opened it, and the pair of pink diamonds, one of which would become the centerpiece of Tia's necklace, tumbled onto the table. "To check it against these."

The king hardly looked at the stones. "Either will match. The colors are the same."

Maria shook her head. "Actually, they're not."

"Of course they are. And your five minutes are—"

But Maria had stopped listening. A trickle of ice water seemed to slip down her spine. She looked at the single light bulb in its overhead socket.

"Is there…?" She cleared her throat. "Is there a way to get more light in this room, sir?"

"No."

"Surely we could take the crown into the display room?"

"Surely we could not," Aegeus said coldly. "And I repeat, your time is— What are you doing?"

Maria's hands were trembling but she tried to stay calm. She put the pair of pink diamonds back in their bag, put the bag in her tote and took out a small flashlight and a jeweler's loupe. Quickly, she put the loupe to her eye and turned on the flashlight.

"Ms. Santos!" The king's voice was sharp. "The Aristan diamond is priceless. I do not want you poking at it and picking at it and—"

"It's a fake!" Her words seemed to explode in the confines of the small room. She looked up, horrified. "This half of the Stefani diamond. What's supposed to be the Stefani diamond. It isn't a diamond at all."

The king's already pale face went paper-white. He shot to his feet. "Give me the crown!"

"Sir. The stone is a fake. Cubic zirconium. Or something else. It's an excellent forgery but…" God, she was shaking like a woman with a high fever! "Your Majesty. I have some tools in my workshop. I can do some tests but I am sure—"

"Give me the crown!" Aegeus roared. He snatched it from her and stuffed it into the velvet bag, but suddenly his eyes grew wide and his face lost what little color it had. A strangled sound broke from his throat; he clapped his hand to his heart, the bag fell on the table and the king tumbled back into his chair.

Maria leaped to her feet, ran to the door and flung it open. "Help!" she shouted. "Please, someone help! The king's collapsed!"

At once, the seemingly empty corridor swarmed with people. Maria fell back against the wall. Someone scooped everything from the table—the loupe, the flashlight and the velvet bag—dumped them into her leather tote, thrust the tote at her, then grasped her arm, hurried her out of the palace and to Alex's waiting limousine.

It wasn't until she was back at the guesthouse that she realized the crown of Aristo had gone home with her.

What did you do when you had absconded with a royal crown?

Maria sat at her workbench, staring blindly at the crown as she tried to come to grips with all that had happened today. The wrenching realization that she was pregnant. The horrifying discovery that the half of the Stefani diamond in the Aristan crown was not a diamond at all and then, the king's collapse.

Was Aegeus dead? Had her news killed him? She'd phoned the palace. Useless. She had the private telephone number of the queen's personal secretary but reached only her voice mail. Desperate for diversion, she'd filled the time running tests on the pink stone in the crown, praying all the while that her initial judgment had been wrong.

She'd done a dozen tests, everything from the silly—did the stone fog when she blew on it?— to the absolutely, completely scientific.

She'd used an electronic tool called a diamond tester. She'd brought it out last, as if by holding off she could avoid the truth. The tester had been one of the things she'd brought with her from New York; she hadn't even been aware she had it with her until now.

The thing was a complex piece of equipment but it was simple to operate. Turn it on, touch the probe at one end of it to a stone. If the stone was a real diamond, a green light came on. If it wasn't…

If it wasn't, nothing happened.

Nothing had happened, half a dozen times.

Maybe the tester wasn't working. That had been her hope.

So she'd touched the probe to every white diamond in the crown. To the diamonds in Tia's almost-completed necklace. To the two big pink stones she'd taken to the palace.

The green light blinked on each time.

Then she'd touched it to the pink stone in the Aristan crown. *Please,* she'd prayed, *please let the green light come on.*

It didn't.

The stone was a brilliant, beautiful fake. It would fool anybody. Anybody but an expert.

Still, maybe she was wrong. Maybe she'd missed something. Was there a test she'd forgotten? Anything was possible, she told herself, and reached for the phone.

Far across the ocean, Joaquin answered on the first ring. "Maria," he said happily, on hearing her voice. "*¿Como se va?* Sela was just saying—"

"Joaquin. I need your help."

He was not a GG—a Graduate Gemologist— as she was. The degree had cost her a small fortune; she was still carrying the debt. But his depth and breadth of knowledge was excellent, and she knew she could trust him with this devastating news. She told him what she'd discovered. Described the tests she'd run. Their conversation grew complex, touched on things like heating, magnification, trigons and dodecahedral surfaces of octahedral crystal formations and then, finally, she took a deep breath and told him she'd used a diamond tester. And the stone had failed that final test.

"You're sure the tester is working properly?"

"I checked the battery. And it gave a green light, literally, to a couple of dozen diamonds, pink and white."

"But not this one."

"No," Maria said, "not this one."

Joaquin's sigh drifted through the telephone. "I don't envy you, *chica*. You are about to be the bearer of very bad news for someone."

She gave a sad little laugh. "I'm afraid I already am."

"Call me if you need me. Sela says to tell you she can do without me for a few days. We both love you, you know that."

She smiled. "Doing without you, even for a few days, is impossible. I love you, too, Joaquin. With all my—"

"How cozy."

Maria spun around. Alexandros stood in the doorway, arms folded, legs apart, face stony and cold.

"Alexandros! I didn't hear you come in."

"No. Obviously not. Don't let me interrupt you, Maria. Not when you're in the middle of an obviously important call."

She said a quick "goodbye" to Joaquin and hung up the phone. Then she slid from the stool and went to her lover. He didn't move. Didn't smile. Didn't react at all when she put her hand on his arm.

"Your father—"

"I know all about my father."

"Is he—is he—"

"He's in the hospital. He had a heart attack." Alex's mouth narrowed. "Thanks to you."

"I never meant—"

"What did you say to him? Did you perhaps tell him you were sleeping with me even though you miss your lover in New York?" His mouth twisted. "No. Why would you do that when you've been so careful to hide that information from me?"

"Alexandros. Listen to me. I don't have—"

"Liar!" He caught her by the shoulders, his hands rough on her tender flesh, and drew her to her toes, just as he had after their first night together. "It's the same man you were talking to that morning three months ago." When she said nothing, his face contorted. "Answer me, damn you! Admit it."

"I was talking with Joaquin, yes. But—"

"Can't you do without him for another few days?"

"Alexandros." Her voice broke. "You're wrong about him."

"I was wrong about you, you mean."

"I told you, Joaquin works for me. He's married."

"What would that matter to a woman like you?"

Maria felt the insult like a knife to the heart. She jerked free of his hands, her face white, eyes glittering with tears.

"I don't deserve that," she whispered.

Yes, he thought, she did. She deserved that and more. He had taken her to his bed. Held her in his arms as she slept. Awakened her with his kisses. He had shared his life with her these past weeks. Fool that he was, he'd come to—to care for her. To want her more than he'd ever wanted anything or anyone in his entire life.

He'd even imagined—he'd stupidly imagined he might keep her with him after her work here was over.

He turned away. Composed himself. She was just another woman. More beautiful, perhaps. More intelligent. More fun. In the end, though, she was the same as all the others. She was with him because of who he was. Because of the power he wielded.

Because he was a prince, not a man. He had to remember that.

She was his mistress, bought and paid for. She was not his lover; she was not in his bed of her own free will but because he had demanded her presence there.

He took a breath and looked at her. "What did you say to my father?" His voice was cold. "He was fine at the start of his meeting with you."

"He wasn't. He looked ill."

"Answer the question. What did you do to make him collapse?"

Maria stared at Alex. He was looking at her as he had not done in weeks, as if he were an autocrat and she were his to command. His expression radiated scorn—and maybe she deserved it. She'd slept with a man who'd made it clear he wanted her sexually, not any other way.

And she'd fallen in love with him.

Wasn't she repeating a pattern for which she'd vilified her mother—up to and including the shame of becoming pregnant?

God. Oh, God! How had she let this happen? And what would she do next? End the pregnancy? Have the baby? Raise it, alone, as her mother had raised her? Because it was only in fairy tales that the handsome prince married the beautiful commoner and lived with her happily ever after.

"I'm waiting, Maria."

She wrapped her arms around herself. Lifted her chin. Forced herself to meet Alex's steely gaze without flinching.

"I told him something about the Aristan crown."

"And?"

"And, it upset him. I'm sorry for that but I was—I was shocked myself and I just blurted it out—"

"Blurted out what? I'm not in the mood for games, Maria."

Maria swallowed dryly. Her lover was a prince of the house of Karedes. He had to know the truth.

"I told him—I told him the half of the Stefani diamond in the crown wasn't real."

For a long moment, nothing happened. Then Alex laughed. The sound startled her.

"You told the king that a stone that is beyond price wasn't real?" His laughter ended as quickly as it had begun. "And he called you, what? A liar? A fool? An idiot? Or all three?"

"It isn't real," Maria said quietly. "It's an excellent fake—but a fake, nevertheless."

Alex's face darkened. "He should have had you thrown out for spouting such nonsense!"

"Listen to me, Alex."

"No, *glyka mou*, you listen to me! I don't know what you thought to accomplish with such a lie but—"

"The stone's counterfeit!" Maria grabbed the crown from the workbench along with a stack of papers and shoved all of it into his hands. "Here's the crown."

"You took it out of the palace?—"

"I didn't plan to take it but… Never mind the details. Look at my notes. I ran endless tests. That's why I phoned Joaquin, to see if maybe, just maybe there was something I missed. There wasn't. The Aristan pink diamond isn't a diamond at all!"

Alex stared at her. Then he began leafing through the papers, quickly at first and then, as he began to absorb what she'd written, more and more slowly. He stared at the crown. At the papers.

Finally, he looked up.

"I don't understand. Who would have done this? And how? The crown's been in the vault for years."

Maria spread her hands. "I have no answers. I only know the diamond is a fake."

Alex put down the papers and the crown, and

ran a hand through his hair. "You're sure? There's no possibility of error?"

"I'm a Graduate Gemologist," she said softly. "I've appraised lots and lots of diamonds. I even did some work with an insurance company that involved fraud and a diamond that would have been worth millions, had it been real." She paused. "I phoned Joaquin because he's knowledgeable. And completely trustworthy."

Alex's mouth thinned. "I'll just bet he is."

"Damn it, stop being a fool! I phoned him that morning in your apartment to tell him I thought I had a good shot at winning the competition because I knew how much it mattered to him and his wife. And I called him now to pick his brain. He's not my lover. He never has been. He's married to my best friend and he's my friend, too. I can trust him to keep quiet about this—or am I wrong, thinking you don't want the citizens of Aristo learning the truth about the diamond from the front pages of the world's newspapers?"

A muscle flickered in Alex's jaw. She was right about the need for discretion. The diamond was priceless, not only as a stone but as a symbol. No Aristan ruler could ever be crowned without it. There was also his grandfather's pronouncement, what everyone called King Christos's Legacy, the pledge that both halves of the Stefani diamond would have to be joined together in the crown of Adamas if ever the two kingdoms, Calista and Aristo, were to be reunited.

And then, he thought, looking at Maria, then there was Maria herself.

Maria, who had brought him the kind of joy he'd never expected to find. What he'd told himself a little while ago was a lie. She'd come to Aristo because he'd forced her to do so, yes, but that was in the past. She was here now because it was what they both wanted. He couldn't imagine ending the day without sharing a few quiet moments with her as they stood in each other's arms, watching the sun set over his beloved island. Couldn't imagine opening his eyes in the morning and not finding her in his arms again.

As for Joaquin… He'd seen his Maria with him but, really, what had he seen? A man putting his arms around a woman. A kiss, but were either the embrace or the kiss those of lovers? Had she lifted her face to Joaquin as she lifted hers to him? Had she drawn Joaquin's head down to hers? Had anything about that kiss held the heat, the power of what happened between his Maria and him?

God, he was a fool. Accusing her of things he knew, in his heart, were not true. Things she would never do. He had to tell her what she'd come to mean to him, that he didn't want her to leave him…

"I only wish," she said brokenly, "I just wish I'd broken the news to your father differently. Perhaps, if I had—"

"It's all right, *glyka mou*."

"No. It isn't. I upset him. His heart—"

"His heart is undamaged. He's at the hospital, yes, but he's awake and alert."

"Thank God," she said, and then she began to weep.

"Ah, sweetheart." Alex gathered her into his arms. "Don't cry."

She wept harder, her face pressed against his shoulder. He could feel her tears dampening his shirt.

"Forgive me for blaming you for what happened. Discovering the stone is fake must have been terrible."

Maria lifted her face to his. "It was horrible. Horrible, Alexandros! I couldn't believe it. That was why I called Joaquin—"

"I spoke before I thought," he said gruffly,

framing her face between his hands. "An old failing, I'm afraid. Ask my brothers. Or my sisters." He smiled. "They'll tell you the same thing. I hear something, I get upset, I react." He clasped her chin, lifted her mouth to his and kissed her. "Will you forgive me?"

Their eyes met, his dark with anguish, hers bright with tears. Would she forgive him? How could she do anything else? She loved this man with all her heart. He had been through an awful shock about his father. She could grant him some leeway, couldn't she?

And she carried his child.

She had to tell him. She knew she did. They had created this tiny life together. No matter what the consequences, Alexandros had the right to know. She was not her mother and he was not a clone of her father.

"Maria? Please, sweetheart, say you'll forgive me."

"You know I will," she said softly, smiling through her tears.

Alex let out a long breath. "*Glyka mou*. We must talk. About us."

"Yes. We do."

"But not now." He held her closer. "The next days are going to be hectic. I'll have to tell my family about the Stefani diamond. We'll have to meet with the council and decide how to handle this. And there's my mother's birthday…"

"Can you postpone the celebration?"

"My father has already said it must go on as scheduled."

"But if he's ill…"

"This is a national celebration, sweetheart. Royal responsibility to the people comes before everything else." He frowned. "And now that I know this about the diamond, I wonder if my father isn't concerned that his illness should not seem too important. You see, if something should happen to him, if a new king had to be crowned… That could not happen unless the real diamond were found and placed in the crown. Do you understand?"

Maria nodded. Like most little girls, she'd loved fairy tales. Now she knew, first-hand, that real kings and queens and princes and princesses did not live such easy lives.

That fairy tales didn't always end happily, she thought, and a shudder went through her.

"What is it, *agapoula mou*?"

"Nothing," she said quickly. "Just—I'm just thinking of how busy everyone will be the next few days."

"We'll manage. I, especially, because I'll have you beside me."

Alex bent to her and kissed her. Whispered soft words against her lips. Her arms crept around his neck. *Now,* she told herself. *Never mind that there's no time for real talking. Let him ask you to stay with him, and you can tell him about the baby—*

His cell phone rang. He blanched as he grabbed it from his pocket.

"*Ne?*" he said brusquely.

But it wasn't the hospital, it was Andreas. The conversation was brief. When it ended, Alex drew her against him.

"I can't stay, sweetheart. I must meet with Sebastian and Andreas. There are many things to discuss, and now is as good a time as any to tell them about the diamond."

She nodded. "Tell them, too, how sorry I am."

"You have nothing to be sorry for, *glyka mou.*" His lips curved in a smile. "But if you feel you must show contrition for some imagined misdeed, I'll consider letting you find creative ways to do so later on."

She laughed and kissed him, and when he whispered something that made her blush, she kissed him again.

"Tonight," she promised.

He gathered up the papers and the Aristan crown; he put his arm around her as they walked to the door.

"Tonight," he said softly.

But one night became another and then another. The mystery of the diamond, the king's illness, the birthday celebration on the horizon... Alex was caught up in the politics of the palace.

There was no time for anything else.

CHAPTER TWELVE

THE day of the queen's birthday celebration was an anomaly.

It was winter, when cool winds and rain often lashed Aristo, but this day dawned bright and warm.

Alex hardly noticed. He had not been home since he'd left Maria in the guesthouse. He'd returned the crown to the display case in the vault and, ever since, he'd been closeted with his brothers.

They were trying to come up with answers. Where was the missing diamond? Who had stolen it? When? How could the switch have gone unnoticed? Where did they start searching for the real stone? Most pressing of all, how could they keep it all a secret?

And it had to be a secret. They could not permit word to get out that the stone was gone.

On the simplest level, news like that would be humiliating. Far more unsettling were the possible political consequences. What if a

Calistan sheikh somehow gained control of the diamond? Could he then twist the true meaning of King Christos's legacy, join the Aristan stone to the one in the Crown of Calista, and claim the right to rule both kingdoms?

It was a real possibility, one that might well destroy Aristo.

He missed Maria terribly. Her smile. Her quiet strength. The feel of her in his arms. He phoned her whenever he could: even the sound of her soft voice was an oasis of calm in the middle of a storm.

"I miss you, *glyka mou*," he told her softly.

She missed him, too. Terribly. But she understood that he was needed at the palace. Sometimes, she could forget her lover was a prince. Now, she couldn't escape it. So, rather than burden him with her own feelings, she did what she thought was right. She said she missed him, too, but she was busy.

"Even if you were here, Alexandros, I couldn't spend time with you. I have last-minute work to do on your mother's necklace."

"Oh," he said, just that one word, but he sounded disappointed. She almost told him she was lying, that she missed him so badly she ached, that if he came through the door she'd toss everything aside and run into his arms...

But the last thing he needed now was a clinging female. Her Alex, along with Sebastian and Andreas, were like jugglers trying to keep a dozen balls in the air. Elissa had just arrived home. She and Kitty were busy helping their mother get ready for the party.

The king had come home from the hospital against the advice of his doctors. The heart attack had not done any damage, true, but they wanted other tests. Nonsense, said Aegeus. There were affairs of state to deal with. Tia's birthday. All the media attention the celebration had brought. Scores of foreign dignitaries.

"I am fine," he insisted.

Was he? The brothers thought their father looked ill.

"Actually," Sebastian said, "he looks like hell."

It was an accurate assessment. The king was pale. He seemed to have shrunk in size and there was a constant sheen of sweat on his forehead. And why did he never mention the missing diamond? That seemed strangest of all.

"If we can just get through the celebration tonight…" Alex said, and they all agreed. Get through tonight and then they could institute a real if subtle search for the missing stone.

Alex was going home to shower and change.

"We'll have half an hour alone, sweetheart," he said when he phoned Maria, "but we can make the most of that half hour." He told her how they'd do that, in explicit detail, and she gave a sexy little sigh and said she'd be waiting.

Smiling, he flipped his cell phone shut. He needed that thirty minutes, not just to make love to her but to tell her what he'd started to tell her three days ago. What he should have told her weeks ago.

He didn't want her to leave him.

Once she gave the necklace to the king, once the king presented it to the queen, Maria would go back to New York.

He could not imagine letting that happen.

They were at the start of their relationship, not the end. In the last month, she had become part of him. She was—she was everything to him. Sometimes, when he held her close, he wanted to tell her—to tell her—

"Alex?" Andreas was hurrying toward him. "Change in plans. Last-minute stuff. Sebastian's meeting with that guy from the BBC, I'm going to talk to CNN. Kitty's doing a piece with *The New York Times*. Lissa was going to deal with *Newsweek* but Mother needs her, something about the flowers. Can you take her spot?"

Alex looked at his watch. "I have to get home, Andreas."

"You mean," his brother said, smiling, "you want to see Maria."

"No, of course not. It's just that my tux is at home…" Alex sighed. "You're right. I do."

"Well, you'll see her soon enough. The party starts in a couple of hours. Let your driver pick up your tux, okay? If you don't take over for Lissa, we'll be up the creek without a paddle."

Alex hesitated, but what choice was there? He couldn't walk away from his duty, no matter what his own needs. He hoped Maria would understand.

She did more than understand. She said that it was just as well, she still had to do her nails and her hair. He said fine, he was glad it had all worked out, but he was lying.

What he'd wanted her to say was that she'd been longing for him. That it was agony to know they would not have half an hour alone.

He had no way of knowing that Maria was lying, too. She'd been counting the hours until Alex came to her, but she couldn't tell him that. She needed the feel of his arms around her. And then there was her pregnancy. She had to find the right time to tell him about it.

But when?

He was, after all, a man with all the responsibilities of a life completely different from hers. He might see her as an exciting lover but that was all she was, all she ever could be…

Her throat tightened.

Maybe she wouldn't tell him about the baby. Not just yet, anyway.

Not until the time was right.

The evening started with a flourish.

A dozen royal heralds played a trumpet fanfare at the top of the marble steps that led into the huge ballroom. A velvet curtain at the far end was drawn back and the queen swept in on the king's arm. The hundreds of guests smiled and applauded her arrival. Every eye was on the radiant Tia.

Every eye but Alex's.

He was waiting at the opposite end of the enormous room, waiting and watching for Maria. Where was she?

"Alexandros," a voice whispered, and he turned and there she was, standing behind him, so gorgeous in a silk gown the color of fine sherry, her dark hair tumbling down her back in a profusion of waves and curls accented with tiny ruby and diamond stars he'd had sent to her, that the sight of her almost stopped his heart.

He didn't think, didn't hesitate but took her hands, drew her through the crowd and out to the terrace, took her in his arms and kissed her.

She melted against him.

"Maria," he said softly, "*kardoula mou*, you are the most beautiful woman in the world."

Her mouth curved against his. "And you, my prince, are the most handsome man on the planet."

He kissed her again. "I hoped you'd be here before the celebration started."

"The car," she said, on a little laugh. "We had a flat tire. Don't let on that you know, Alex. Poor Alastor felt awful."

"As he should," Alex said, but he smiled. "Never mind. You're here now. That's what matters. Did you give the necklace to my father?"

Maria nodded. "He seemed pleased with it. He said he'll give it to your mother at midnight." She hesitated. "Is he all right? He looks—"

"Terrible. I know. We tried to convince him to cancel but he refused." Alex gathered her closer against him. "Let's not talk about that," he said softly. "Not when I have something important to discuss with you."

Now was the time to say that she did, too.

"Maria." Gently, he brushed a curl from her forehead. "I know you're supposed to... I mean, I know we agreed you would..." Alex groaned. "I'm making a mess of this, *glyka mou*. What I'm trying to say is—"

"Your Highness! Prince Alexandros!"

An equerry was running toward them. Alex knew, before the man said another word, that the news was of his father.

"The king?"

The equerry nodded. "He's been taken ill, sir."

Alex ran into the ballroom. Maria hiked up her skirt and ran at his side.

"Where is he?"

"The throne room, sir. There's a helicopter on its way. Your Highness?" The equerry, running with them, caught Alex by the sleeve just before they reached the throne room. The simple action was so unprecedented that it startled even Maria. "The king wishes to see Ms. Santos." He swallowed audibly. "Alone."

"Me?" Maria said, in amazement. "That can't be."

The Karedes family was gathered outside the closed doors of the throne room, faces white and puzzled. When Maria hesitated, the queen motioned her forward.

"My husband wants to see you, Ms. Santos." Tia bit her lip. "Please. I don't think there's time to waste."

"Go on," Alex said softly, and touched his hand to her cheek.

The doors closed behind her with an audible click.

This was Maria's first visit to the throne room. It was not as big as she'd imagined, the size, perhaps, of half her loft, but it was elegant. A red carpet stretched toward a pair of ornate chairs that stood on a raised platform but the chairs— presumably, the thrones—were empty.

"Here," a weak voice said.

The king was alone. He lay on a crimson velvet sofa, head elevated on a blue silk pillow.

Maria moved slowly toward him. Her heart thumped. *He's dying,* she thought, and, as if he'd read her mind, Aegeus struggled up against the pillow.

"I am not dead yet, Ms. Santos. Come forward."

"Your Majesty. Your family is outside. Surely, you want to see them—"

"You were not supposed to learn that the diamond in the crown is false."

Maria caught her breath. "You knew?"

The king's face contorted. He groaned and

Maria swung toward the door to call for help but Aegeus's fingers wrapped around her wrist with the steely grip of command.

"My son is in love with you."

She stared at him. "What?"

"Alexandros loves you, Ms. Santos. I'm not sure he knows it yet, but he does." He drew a rasping breath. "But you must not return that love."

Maria shook her head. "Your Majesty. Please. You're very sick—"

"All the more reason for you to pay attention to what I say," he said, a touch of the old sharpness edging his words. "You must understand that there is no room in a royal's life for love."

"Sir. This is hardly the time—"

"A prince is not born to his mother or father, Ms. Santos, he is born to his nation and his people. His life, from birth, is one of responsibility. Commitment. Obligation." Aegeus took another labored breath. "Someday, my sons will marry. They will marry young women born of blood as royal as theirs, young women who understand what is expected of them."

Maria sank to her knees beside the sofa. She could feel the sting of tears in her eyes and she blinked furiously to keep them from falling.

"I love your son," she whispered. "And I

understand he has responsibilities. I can help him shoulder them. I can step back when I must."

"If you truly love him, you will give him up."

"No. No! You can't ask that of me. Or of him. If Alexandros loves me—"

"His duty is to his people. To his mother. To me. A prince who falls in love with the wrong woman can only destroy her. He can only destroy his nation and himself. Maria. If you love my son as you say you do, you will leave him. And you will not tell him the reason. Alexandros must never know you love him, or that you gave him up because you love him. You must walk away from him, from his life, and never look back."

Tears streamed down Maria's face.

"You ask too much of me," she said. "You have no right!"

"I love my country and my people. And though you may not think so, I love my children." The king took a long, agonizing breath. "Alex thinks you will make him happy but you won't, Maria. Your love can only hurt him. You must, you *must*, set him free."

"Your Majesty—"

The king jerked upright. His hand went to his

throat; his breath rattled though a mouth gone wide, gasping for air.

Maria sprang to her feet.

"Help," she shouted.

"Maria," Aegeus whispered hoarsely.

"Someone, help—"

The door swung open. Footsteps clattered against the marble floor. And, as they did, Aegeus grabbed Maria's hand again.

"Promise me," he said fiercely. "Swear that you will do what you know you must."

Weeping, Maria stared at the king's stricken face—and knew he was right. She could not share Alexandros's life. He was a prince and she—she was nobody.

"I swear," she said.

A smile pulled Aegeus's lips back from his teeth—and then he fell back against the pillows. His family surrounded him. The queen sank to the floor beside him, took his hand and began to weep.

"He's gone," she said, "he's gone!"

Alex gently drew her to her feet. Sebastian put his arm around her. Andreas touched her shoulder. Kitty and Lissa bent over their father and sobbed.

And Maria did the only thing she could. The

thing Aegeus had asked of her. The promise she had made him that she knew, in her heart of hearts, was right.

She slipped from the room, from the palace.

From Alexandros's life.

CHAPTER THIRTEEN

A MONARCH'S death left behind a void that must be filled quickly for the safety and stability of the kingdom and its people.

At first, all was confusion.

Despite Aegeus's illness, his death had been sudden. The king's private physicians tried every possible means to revive him but to no avail. The Karedes family clustered around the king's lifeless body; the palace, filled with guests for the queen's birthday celebration, buzzed with rumors. Andreas comforted his sisters. Sebastian, who as eldest son would, within hours, be named the Prince Regent, was immediately surrounded by guards whose duty it was to protect him, especially in times of turmoil. Alex held his mother in his arms.

Through it all—the loss of his father, his mother's tears, his sister's sobs, the stunned reactions of his brothers and his own shock—through all that, Alex found himself looking over the heads of those who'd crowded into the room.

Where was Maria? He needed her. And, surely, she needed him. She'd been alone with his father at the moment of his death.

She needed his comfort. His arms. And he, God, he needed her.

A reporter and a couple of photographers had somehow slipped into the room; two of the guards were hustling them out. Had those guards, in error, forced Maria aside?

He was desperate to find her but Tia was distraught. He couldn't leave her, not until she was calmer. He told himself not to worry. His Maria was smart. She was resourceful. She'd find his car, have his driver take her home. Or she'd wait for him in a quiet corner of the palace.

Soon, he'd be alone with her. And he'd tell her what he now knew had been in his heart for weeks. He loved her. He adored her. He could not imagine life without her.

He didn't just want her to stay here, on Aristo, as his lover.

He wanted her to become his wife.

One thing about death, he thought as he led his mother from the room. It had a profound way of making a man see what really mattered.

And what mattered, the only thing that mattered, was Maria.

* * *

In the face of a nation's grief and loss, tradition became its solace.

Aegeus would lie in state for three days. The Accession Council would meet to formally name Sebastian the Prince Regent, though by tradition coupled with the decades-old decree of Christos, there could be no coronation of him as king until the missing half of the Stefani diamond was returned to the Aristan crown. The Privy Council would meet, too, so its members could certify the succession declaration.

Andreas took on the coordination of those meetings. Sebastian immersed himself in policy conferences. It fell to Alex to finalize plans for the royal funeral. And yet, as he raced home just before dawn, his thoughts were not on any of those things. He was consumed by worries over something far more important.

Maria.

She hadn't been waiting for him in the palace, not in the public rooms or in the royal apartments. His driver *was* waiting, in the courtyard, and in response to Alex's questions the man could only shake his head and say that he had not seen Ms. Santos.

Alex checked his cell phone. Again. He'd already done that a dozen times but maybe, now, she'd left a message… She hadn't. He'd phoned her endlessly and been connected to her voice mail, where he'd gone from leaving messages telling her he would break away as soon as he possibly could to increasingly terse ones asking her to contact him.

By the time he reached the house on the bay, he was frantic.

"Maria?" he shouted as he burst through the door. "Maria?"

No answer. He ran up the stairs to his bedroom, flung open the door. The room was dark. Empty.

"Maria," he said again, and flew down the stairs, almost stumbling over Athenia who stood at the bottom wearing a housecoat, her hair in curlers.

"Your Highness. Our hearts are filled with grief. We are all so sorry for you—"

"Yes. Thank you. Where is Ms. Santos?"

Athenia bit her lip. Shook her head. Alex cursed in frustration—and then breathed a sigh of relief. He knew where Maria would be. In the guesthouse. He knew her habits. She was probably losing herself in work.

But the guesthouse, Maria's workshop, stood as silent and empty as his bedroom. Something about that silence made his heart rise in his throat. He ran back to the main house, took the steps two at a time, flung open the bedroom door, this time switched on the light…

And knew, instantly, that Maria was gone.

The room felt cold. Not just empty but barren, as if the very life had been stripped from it. He went to the dressing room, stepped inside. Her suitcase was gone. The beautiful clothes he'd bought her hung from the racks like mournful reminders of the past.

"Maria," Alex said, bewildered. What the hell had happened? Where was his Maria? He turned in a slow circle—and saw the envelope propped on the bed. "Alex," it said, and that it didn't say Alexandros was a statement in itself.

He picked it up. Opened it. Withdrew the note inside and read it. It was brief. She was, she said, terribly sorry for his loss. Though she'd only met his father a handful of times, she'd come to respect him. She'd wanted to tell him that herself but…

The "but" made Alex's belly knot.

But, she wrote, she knew that the king's death meant Alex would be immersed in the duties of a prince. She saw no reason to burden him with concern for her, especially since she was returning to New York anyway, now that her duties here were completed.

Her duties here.

He looked up, his face a mask of disbelief. Was that what it had been? Had sleeping with him been part of her duties? Was leaving him such a relief that she couldn't have waited to say goodbye?

He read the note again. And again. Then he let out a roar of anguished rage from a place in his soul he'd never known existed, and tore the note into a dozen pieces.

A state funeral was not a simple thing.

Fortunately, plans for events like this had always existed. Except for the addition of a motorcade, those plans had not changed much since the time of the Crusades.

Aegeus lay in state for three days while his people, friends, relatives and foreign heads of state all paid their respects.

The Sheikh King Zakari Al'Farisi represented the island of Calista.

Zakari, a proud and ruthless man, made all the appropriate comments to the press; he offered Tia his polite condolences.

In private talks with the Karedes princes,

however, Zakari's words were probing as well as troubling.

He seemed to know that Aristo's half of the Stefani diamond was missing.

Though Alex, Andreas and Sebastian had met with their council and agreed the mystery had to be kept secret until it was solved, that decision was—as Andreas wryly put it—pretty much the equivalent of shutting the stable door after the horse had been stolen.

Clearly, the news had reached Calista. And that was dangerous. Since Sebastian could not be crowned without the true diamond, Alex's worry—that it might fall into the wrong hands and a Calistan prince could take the Aristan throne—seemed more and more plausible.

Added to concerns of state were those of family. Lissa and Kitty took their father's death hard and clung to Andreas. Tia, shocked by her loss, claimed Alex for solace and support. Sebastian, now the Prince Regent, was, by custom, designated to lead them all through the necessary formalities.

Alex had no time to think, or told himself he had no time for it. But at night, when the hands of his watch seemed to slow to a crawl, he lay awake in his palace rooms, despising Maria, despising himself, telling himself what a fool he'd been to have imagined himself in love with her because he certainly had not loved her.

Of course, he hadn't.

He counted down the days until the formalities of mourning would end. He had work to do, investors to meet with and reassure that nothing would change on Aristo. He was also fully involved in organizing the search for the missing diamond. Once the mourning period was behind him, he'd be far too busy to think about Maria Santos.

A lie.

Life slowly returned to normal. He was busy from early morning until late at night. And he thought about her all the time.

What he needed was closure, to tell her, to her face, that she had meant nothing more to him than he had obviously meant to her, but that would mean seeking her out and he wasn't about to lower himself to that.

Strangely, no one in his family asked about Maria until one morning, when his mother phoned and invited him to breakfast. He was incredibly busy that day but he knew Tia's grief was still new; nothing would have made him refuse her request.

They chatted briefly about nothing special—

and then, without warning, Tia asked why Maria had gone.

"Why wouldn't she?" Alex said, with a shrug. "She finished your necklace. Her work was over."

"I'm not talking about her work," Tia said. "I'm talking about the feelings you and she have for each other."

"You're wrong, Mother. We had no—"

"Alex. I'm your mother. I'm also a woman. I know love when I see it. Maria and you were in love. So, why did you let her go?"

Alex thought of half a dozen answers, all of which would have worked and, instead, found himself speaking the truth.

"I didn't," he said in a low voice. "She left me. She enjoyed—she enjoyed our time together but—"

"Nonsense. She loves you. I saw it. Everyone saw it."

"The hell she did!" Alex shot to his feet. "She left the night Father died. What was I supposed to do? Go after her? Walk out on my duties to try and convince her not to leave me?"

"Your duties," Tia said softly. "Yes. Such things always get in the way." She looked up at him. "Had you ever told her you loved her?"

His mouth thinned. "No."

"Perhaps," she said carefully, "perhaps you should have."

Yes, Alex thought, he should have. He'd known the truth, in his heart. Why hadn't he faced it sooner? Now it was too late.

"It's never too late," his mother said, and he realized he'd spoken aloud. "Alexandros. Love is a precious gift. Don't throw it away."

"How do you know that, Mother? I know you respected Father but I don't believe you truly loved him." Alex drew a ragged breath. "Hell," he said softly, "I'm sorry. I shouldn't have—"

"You spoke the truth, my son. I didn't truly love Aegeus, nor did he truly love me." The queen's eyes shone with unshed tears. "And that's exactly the reason you must not let love slip through your fingers, Alexandros. Even a royal is entitled to happiness."

The New York weather was harsh and uninviting.

Snow, slush, sleet and grey skies were daily companions. The sun seemed reluctant to put in even a cursory appearance. The weather was a reflection of Maria's despair. She was lonely for Alexandros, for Aristo, for the happiness she had found with him there.

It was good that she was busy. Shops that had not wanted any part of her in the past clamored for her designs. *L'Orangerie* headed the list.

And, well, yes, there was one other good thing. A miraculous thing that had, at first, terrified her and now made her heart sing with joy.

A visit to her doctor had confirmed that she was pregnant. She was carrying Alex's child. A little girl, Sela had said, smiling.

"Morning sickness at the beginning of your pregnancy. And look how high you're carrying. Absolutely, a girl."

Maria didn't believe in the old superstitions but it didn't matter. She would love her baby whatever the sex, and she would name it for Alexandros even though he was gone from her life.

He, and Aristo, were moving forward. Sebastian was the Prince Regent, though there was no mention of the missing diamond. She'd followed the funeral on TV. The royal family had looked saddened but composed. Alex had been his mother's strong, handsome escort.

Just seeing him had made Maria's throat constrict.

She would never stop loving him.

But she would have his daughter to love. It saddened her that her baby would never know her daddy but when Alexandra was old enough, she'd tell her what a fine man he was, what a loving man, what a good man—and never mind that he hadn't called or written or tried to find out how she was, where she was…

"Maria? You okay?"

She looked up at Joaquin, working at the end of the bench. He and Sela had been wonderful. Though they knew about the baby, they hadn't asked questions. A good thing, too, because if they had, she might have broken down and wept.

Tears filled her eyes and dripped onto the wax she was working.

"Maria?"

"Yes," she said briskly, wiping the back of her hand across her eyes and flashing a smile, "I'm fine. I just—I think I got a bit of wax in my eye."

"Want me to do that mold?"

"No. No, thanks. I'm almost finished. You know, it's getting late. Why don't we call it a day, hmm?"

"Well, if that's okay… I promised Sela I'd pick up some stuff from the Chinese market on the way home."

"Better get going, then, before the market closes."

Joaquin nodded, cleaned up his end of the

workbench, then put on his coat. He kissed her cheek and she managed to keep the tears from building again until the door closed behind him.

Why was she weeping? She'd wanted to end things cleanly. To keep Alex from contacting her. And she'd succeeded.

She just had to stop crying every five minutes. Sela said it was her hormones. It wasn't. It was her inability to accept that she would never lie in her lover's arms again, but she'd sooner have died than admit that to Sela or even to herself because it wasn't true, it wasn't true, she had a wonderful, fulfilling life now and—

Someone knocked at the loft door.

Maria grabbed the edge of her work-apron and wiped her eyes. Had Joaquin forgotten something? Why didn't he use his key? Unless it was a reporter. They were still driving her crazy, hoping for an interview about life on Aristo and the death of its king.

The knock came again. She sighed, smoothed down her apron, fixed a polite smile to her lips and marched to the door.

"Yes?" No answer. Maria rolled her eyes. "Look, I've said I won't do interviews so whoever you are—"

"Open the door, Maria."

Her heart leaped. No. It couldn't be.

"Maria. Did you hear me? Open this door."

She shook her head, as if Alex could see her. "Go away," she said in a shaky voice.

"I'm not going anywhere. Either you open this door or I'll break it down."

He would, too. He was angry—she could hear it in his voice, and she remembered what his anger had been like that night he'd first come here.

Bam! The door, heavy as a chunk of steel, shuddered under the blow.

"I don't want to see you." Maria licked her lips. "Joaquin is here. He says—"

"He says I've been a fool. And he's right."

Maria stared at the door. "You talked to Joaquin?"

"Just now. On the stairs." Alex's voice softened; she had to put her ear to the door to hear him. "He's been a good friend to you. You're lucky to have him to turn to. Maria, *glyka mou*, let me in."

She swallowed hard. Then she undid the bolt and opened the door.

"I don't want to talk to you," she started to say, but the sight of her Alexandros, so tall, so powerful, so much the lover she remembered, stole the words away. To her horror, her eyes flooded with the tears she'd fought only minutes before. She couldn't let him see her cry, she couldn't, she told herself, and she slapped her hands against the door and started to push it closed.

Alex was too quick. He jammed his shoulder between the door and its frame and pushed. Maria staggered back, the door swung open and he stepped into the loft.

He'd had plenty of time to consider how he would handle this meeting. The flight from Aristo had taken longer than usual. Bad weather had meant putting down at Charles de Gaulle Airport in Paris for a few hours. Just as well, he'd thought. The delay had given him extra time to decide what to say.

He'd come up with a list of questions. A little speech, though he tried not to call it that, in which he'd let Maria know that a woman did not simply walk out on him without explanation.

He would be cautious in expressing his feelings, never mind his mother's insistence that Maria and he were in love. The sad truth, as Tia had admitted, was that his mother didn't know a damned thing about love. If Maria loved him, why had she left him?

A woman who loved a man didn't walk out on him without so much as a handshake.

He wasn't so sure about loving her, either. Why would a man love a woman who'd abandoned him? Who was so independent? Why would he want her back in his life?

Logical, all of it. The trouble was, the closer he'd come to her street, the harder his heart had beaten. All his hours of planning and doubt had dissolved like cotton candy in the rain. And when he'd bumped into a man on the stairs, he'd known instinctively it was Joaquin—and known, just as instinctively, that the guy knew who he was, too, and wanted nothing more than to flatten him.

He could hardly blame him.

Hell, it was what he'd have done if the situation were reversed.

The men had taken a long look at each other.

"Are you the prince?" Joaquin had finally growled. At Alex's nod, the other man's mouth had thinned. "She loves you, you jerk. And you don't deserve her."

Alex had grinned. Then he'd put his hand out.

"You're right," he'd said, and after a few seconds Joaquin had smiled. They'd shaken hands. Then Joaquin had stepped aside and Alex had continued up the stairs to Maria's door when terror had stopped him cold. Certain of everything, sure of nothing, he had resorted to anger…

And then he'd come to his senses.

He would do whatever it took to win his Maria's heart…and, looking into her eyes, he knew, with a rush of fierce joy, that her heart had always been his for the taking.

Maria loved him. He loved her. And he'd be damned if he'd lose her again.

So, in the end, there were no questions, no speeches, no doubts. There was only a man, baring his soul by stepping forward and opening his arms to a woman. And *thank you, God*— there was the woman, his Maria, giving a little cry and throwing herself into his embrace.

He kissed her. Kissed her for a very long time. Her mouth. Her eyes. Her hair.

"Why did you leave me?" he said.

"Because I have no place in your life," she said, returning each kiss, each caress, each sigh.

"I love you. You *are* my life."

Her heart soared, but she shook her head. "I can't be."

"Do you love me?"

How could she lie to him? How could she deny what burned in her heart?

"Yes," she said softly, "I love you. I adore you,

Alexandros. But I can't be part of your life. I—
I'm not cut out to be a mistress."

"Of course you aren't," Alex said, in that imperious way that she'd learned to love. "You're going to marry me and be my wife."

His words were more precious than any of the diamonds in the Aristan crown. She knew she would cherish them forever, even if what he'd just told her could never happen.

"I can't marry you," she whispered.

"Because?"

"Because you're a prince. You have obligations. Duties."

"I have nothing, unless I have you, *glyka mou*. You are my heart. My joy. My love."

Oh, how easy it would be to give in. To say, 'Yes, I'll marry you…' But she couldn't. She loved her Alexandros too much to ruin his life.

"Alexandros, listen to me. Your father's words to me were true."

Alex's eyes darkened. "What are you talking about?"

"The night he died—Aegeus said—he said I was wrong for you. That if I loved you, I had to leave you. He said—"

"Was that why he wanted to see you?" Alex's tone was harsh. "To tell you to go away?"

"No. Yes. It was more than that. He said he wanted the best for you."

"*You* are the best for me, *glyka mou.*"

"Also—also, I think he knew something about the diamond. I think—I think he had something to do with switching the fake for the real one."

"I don't care about that diamond right now," Alex said fiercely. "All that matters is us. What we feel for each other, the life we'll create together... What?"

Maria was laughing. Or maybe she was crying. He couldn't tell; he only knew that something in what he'd just said had affected her.

And then, he knew.

Slowly, he clasped her shoulders. Held her just far enough away so he could look at her from head to toe. She looked different. Her face was fuller. So were her breasts. And, under her denim work-apron, he could see the delicate but clear convexity of her belly.

It all came together. Her nausea. Her exhaustion. And now, these physical changes that made her even more beautiful.

"Maria." He could feel the smile starting to stretch across his lips. "Maria, my heart, my soul, are you pregnant?"

She stared at him. She could lie. She could say, no, of course not…

"Yes," she said softly.

Alex grinned. Then he gathered her in his arms and rained kisses on her face.

"Pregnant," he said, as if he were the first man in the world ever to hear such news. "My God, sweetheart, we're pregnant!" He held her inches from him, his eyes searching hers. "Say the words, Maria. Tell me that you love me as I love you, and that you will do me the honor of becoming my wife."

Maria thought of how far they had come, of a time her Alexandros would have demanded to know if he was really the father of the baby in her womb. She thought of how he had crossed the ocean to claim her. She thought of King Aegeus's warning, and how cold and empty the life he'd foreseen for his son now seemed.

"Alexandros," she said, because if life wasn't worth risks, what was the point? "Alexandros. I love you. And it is you who do me honor, my beloved, by asking me to marry you."

Alex gave her a solemn look. "Is that," he said carefully, "a yes?"

Maria laughed, though she was crying again, this time tears of joy that streamed down her face.

"Yes," she said, "yes, yes, yes!"

Her Alexandros kissed her. Then he kicked the door shut, swept her into his arms, and carried her to the bed.

millsandboon.co.uk Community

Join Us!

The Community is the perfect place to meet and chat to kindred spirits who love books and reading as much as you do, but it's also the place to:

- Get the inside scoop from authors about their latest books
- Learn how to write a romance book with advice from our editors
- Help us to continue publishing the best in women's fiction
- Share your thoughts on the books we publish
- Befriend other users

Forums: Interact with each other as well as authors, editors and a whole host of other users worldwide.

Blogs: Every registered community member has their own blog to tell the world what they're up to and what's on their mind.

Book Challenge: We're aiming to read 5,000 books and have joined forces with The Reading Agency in our inaugural Book Challenge.

Profile Page: Showcase yourself and keep a record of your recent community activity.

Social Networking: We've added buttons at the end of every post to share via digg, Facebook, Google, Yahoo, technorati and de.licio.us.

www.millsandboon.co.uk